BED AND BURIED

TRASH TO TREASURE COZY MYSTERIES, BOOK 1

DONNA CLANCY

SUMMER PRESCOTT BOOKS PUBLISHING

CHAPTER ONE

"Please tell me you are not going to pick through that trash sitting on the side of the road?" Gabby asked her best friend who was pulling her cargo van over to the curb.

"Of course, I am. Do you see that headboard? That will make a beautiful bench," Sage said, excited at the prospect of starting a new project. "And those four chairs will be easy to flip and sell once they are painted and reupholstered with a trendy fabric."

"Don't just sit there," Sage said. "Get out and help me load this stuff in the back of my van."

"You are on your own. I'll be waiting right here until you are done," Gabby replied. "I am not going to be seen scrounging through someone's garbage."

"Fine. I'll do it myself," Sage said. "There was a time you were a fun person and not such a killjoy."

"Yard sales, flea markets and estate sales are fine," Gabby said, leaning out the van window. "I draw the line at piles of trash on the side of the road."

"You know the old saying, someone else's trash," Sage started. "I'm looking at three to four hundred dollars here using free materials and putting in a few hours of work."

"I believe you. You're a great flipper and can always make something out of nothing," Gabby stated. "I wish I had your eye for useful junk."

"I'm glad you don't. I wouldn't have an awesome hairdresser if you did," Sage replied from the back of the van, throwing the last of the four chairs in and closing the door.

Sage Fletcher and Gabby Rhodes had been best friends since middle school when Gabby's family moved to town. Both were athletic and had played on the field hockey and volleyball teams together during high school.

Gabby went on to beauty school since she had a natural talent for cutting and styling hair. Sage had no interest in attending college and went into business for herself. She, too, had a natural talent, but it involved flipping other people's unwanted items and selling her flips online and in her mother's shop, *This and That*. Her creative eye had no bounds, and her business flourished.

"I'm going to drop these off at my workshop before we go to lunch," Sage said. "I have to pick up a set of wall sconces that I need to drop off at my mom's shop."

"I'd love to see your mom. She's always so happy and bubbly when she is at her shop," Gabby stated. "I have a full hope chest thanks to her, and the wedding is still two years away."

"She can sell honey to a bee," Sage said, laughing.

"Even Rory loves to poke around her shop. He's picked up some cool, old tools that he displays in his contractor's office, not to mention all the fishing poles he's bought there," Gabby said, rolling her eyes.

Rory Nash was Gabby's fiancé. He graduated the year ahead of them and opened his own construction company, following in his father's footsteps. They met when Gabby's father hired his company to build a house on the adjacent property as a gift to his daughter for graduating from beauty school. They started dating as the house was being built, and two years later, he proposed.

Sage, on the other hand, went through a difficult

breakup about a year ago and had no interest in finding anyone at the present. She was enjoying her time being single.

"Here we are," Sage said, pulling up to her oversized garage that she had turned into a workshop. "This will only take a minute."

She unlocked the door and propped it open. Turning around, Gabby was standing there with the headboard.

"Oh, yeah, you help here but not in public where anyone can see you," Sage said, teasing her friend.

"Hey, if anyone drives by your driveway they can see me from the street," Gabby said in her own defense.

"You're too funny. Put that against the wall in the far corner," Sage directed.

"These came out gorgeous," Gabby said, holding up one of the sconces. "These would look phenomenal on either side of the fireplace in my living room."

"Sorry, already spoken for," Sage said, setting the last of the four chairs in front of her work bench. "Those little babies used to be carriage lanterns and cost me a whole ten dollars. They are being sold for one hundred and twenty-five. My mom gets twenty percent for her shop commission, and I pocket a nice profit."

"I'm sure you could find something similar and give them to me as a wedding present?"

"Along with all the other things you have requested as wedding gifts?" Sage asked, giving her friend a hard time.

"I haven't wanted that much, have I?" she asked, frowning. "And if I have, it's just because I love everything you create."

"You are so great for my ego," Sage said, picking up the sconces and wrapping them in bubble wrap. "Don't worry, you'll get something amazing for your wedding."

"I know I will, but there is no law against me shopping between now and then," her friend said, looking around.

Sage packed the wrapped sconces in a box and set them in the back of her van. Ten minutes later, they were at her mother's shop. Opening the front door, the friends could hear Sarah Fletcher on the phone arguing with whoever was on the other end. Slamming the phone down on the cradle, she turned to see her daughter and best friend wide eyed at what was said on the one side of the conversation that they could hear.

"Mom, is everything okay?"

"Does it sound like it is okay? That man is going to be the death of me," her mother answered.

"What man?" Sage asked.

"Mr. Peterson, next door. He filed a complaint with the town this morning that the storage trailer that I just had delivered is a foot over the property line."

"Is it?" Gabby asked.

"Of course not. The last time he complained, I had a survey done on the land. The surveyors hammered in orange wooden stakes where the property line lies. I have him on video out there at night pulling the stakes and moving them closer to the shop. He's claiming a good ten feet of my property for his own."

"Why is he being such a jerk?"

"Why? Because he wants to buy the lot of land the store is on. He is trying to force me out of business by constantly trying to find something that I will get in trouble for with the town."

"What does he want your land for?"

"He doesn't want it for anything. He just doesn't like the noise the shop creates by being here. He wants to tear the shop down and leave the land vacant."

"But you were here first," Gabby said. "Didn't he just buy that place not even a year ago?"

"Exactly. My shop has been here for thirty years, and I never had a problem until he moved in next door. The previous neighbors, Mr. and Mrs. Gibson, were such nice people."

"I remember them. During the summer, they used to come over to visit, and we would sit out front drinking lemonade and playing Go Fish."

"Unfortunately, they passed away, and their son sold the house to Mr. Peterson. It's been a nightmare ever since."

"You said you had him on video moving the surveyor's stakes. Have you turned the proof over to the police?"

"I have, and they said there isn't much they can do about it. They told me to move them back and mark the ground with fluorescent paint where they are supposed to be. Every time I go out to do it, he comes out of his house screaming and threatening me. The last time I had the police on my cell phone, and they heard him," Sarah said.

"Did they do anything?" Gabby asked.

"They went to his house to speak to him, and he had the nerve to tell them I was the one that was threatening him, and his wife backed him up. They quickly changed their tunes when the police told them they had been on the phone and heard the whole situation as it unfolded."

"So, what happened?"

"The police told him to leave the surveyor stakes alone and to stay away from me and my shop. The old goat was none too happy."

"I take it by that phone call that he hasn't followed the advice the police gave him the last time they visited him," Sage said. "What are you going to do?"

"Apparently, there isn't much I can do unless he physically hurts me or does property damage. I can file for a restraining order, but you and I both know how good those things work," her mother replied, referring to Sage's old boyfriend.

"Just be careful. He doesn't appear to be all there," Sage said.

"I will. My shop will still be here when that old goat is dead and buried."

"You have to be careful. I wouldn't say that in front of too many customers or in front of Mr. Peterson or his wife. They will take it as a threat and call the police," Gabby said.

"I'm sure they would," Sarah said, unwrapping the sconces. "These are beautiful. The Snows going to love them."

"Not as much as I love them. I wanted them for my house," Gabby said, frowning.

"You want everything that Sage creates," Sarah said, rolling her eyes.

"I said the same thing to her earlier today," Sage said, laughing.

"Gabby, don't forget I have a ten o'clock hair appointment with you tomorrow. The grays are taking over, and I need a trim," Sarah said.

"Same color as last time?"

"Yes, please. I swear having red hair keeps me young. I feel so good about myself when I leave your shop."

"We aim to please," Gabby replied.

"We have to go. I want to be there early for that big yard sale at Fulton Farms. I can usually find some great buys there, and this time, I have a helper to carry stuff."

"It's my day off, and what am I doing? Carrying stuff," Gabby said, smiling at her best friend. "Let's go. At least it's not trash picking like you tried to make me do earlier."

They walked out the front door, and Sarah told the girls to hold on a minute. She ran back into the shop and returned with a credit card for Sage.

"In case you find something good for the shop at the sale," she said.

"Hey, woman! I told you to move that trailer off my property. If you don't, I'll move it, and you won't like where I move it to," Mr. Peterson yelled from his front porch. "This is your last warning."

"Mom, don't say a word," Sage said as her mother got ready to yell back. "Stay here."

Sage marched over to where the neighbor was standing. She planted her feet and put her hands on her hips.

"Just what is your problem?" she asked.

"Figures. The redheaded bimbo can't speak for herself and sends a girl to do her dirty work," Peterson yelled loudly enough for Sarah to hear.

"That redheaded bimbo is my mother, and you better watch what you say about her. She's had that business for over thirty years and is very well liked in this town. Which is more than I can say for you."

"Mouthy, just like her," he yelled. "She won't be in business much longer; I'll see to that."

Flora made her way out the door and stood just behind Ralph. Then she moved forward standing with her hands on her hips next to him. She glared at Sage.

"Get off our property! It seems to run in your

family to go where you are not wanted," she said to Sage.

"If we are handing out warnings, here's mine to you. Leave my mother alone and stay off our property. The police know you are moving the property line stakes and have the video to prove it."

"Do you think I am afraid of the police?" he asked. "They are a joke."

At this point, a small crowd of customers had gathered in front of *This and That* and were watching the exchange between the Petersons and Sage. Most of Sarah's regular customers knew of the trouble she was having with the cranky neighbor and had offered time and time again to be witnesses for her if she had to go in front of any town board.

"Sage! Come on, you have to go, or you'll be late," Sarah yelled to her daughter.

"Listen to your mommy, and get off my property," he said, gritting his teeth. "In the house, Flora, now!"

"Thank you for more ammunition for my mother. You have just been recorded," Sage yelled, holding up her phone as they went into the house and slammed the door.

Sage returned to the shop and was surprised to see the crowd that had gathered there. The Snows were there to pick up their sconces and congratulated Sage on sticking up to the bully on her mother's behalf.

"My son Stephen lives on the other side of Cupston. Mr. Peterson used to live on the next street over from him but directly behind his house. It took almost three years, but the neighborhood banded together and fought him in everything they could to get rid of him. He finally sold his house and moved. Many people had to pay town fines because of him. He has multiple enemies. I'm just sorry that it was Sarah who got stuck living next to him this time. It seems he has gotten worse since the move."

"She seems just as bad," Sage commented. "I think the world would be a better place if they were dead."

"Sage!" Sarah exclaimed. "That's a terrible thing to say."

"She's only saying out loud what other people in this town are thinking, Sarah. Flora can be a miserable person when she wants to be, too. They are made for each other," Mrs. Snow replied. "Anyway, we're here for our sconces. Are they done?"

"They are, and they're inside. And if you don't like them, I know another buyer who does," Sage said, glancing sideways at Gabby.

"I'm sure we are going to love them. Sorry, Gabby."

"That's okay. I still have plenty of time to pick out a wedding gift from our talented flipper here."

"Speaking of flipping, my aunt died, and they are cleaning out her house on Saturday. Would you like to go and grab stuff you can use to create some new items, Sage? No charge. Just go and help yourself to whatever you want."

"Would I? Free is my favorite word."

"Here is my business card. I wrote my aunt's address on the back. I will be there by eight a.m. to oversee things, so you can show up any time after that. Make sure your van is empty. My aunt has some great stuff in her house, but I don't have room for any of it in my home. I am her only living relative, and I have already taken the personal things that I wanted. Gabby and Sarah, you are welcome to come, too. I'm sure you can find some things for the shop and maybe that new house of yours, Gabby. Whatever is left will go to Fulton Farm the following weekend for their next sale."

"Thank you, I can't wait," Sage said, taking the card and tucking it in her pocket.

The two friends climbed up into Sage's van and left for Fulton Farm. Twice a year, the owners held a huge yard sale on their property, and Sage made sure to attend each time. She could fill her van with lots of buys at cheap prices. People from all over Cupston donated items for the sale throughout the year, and the proceeds from the sale not only kept the farm going but also benefited local charities. This time the Cupston Animal Rescue League had been named as the recipient.

The ride to the farm only took twenty minutes. The huge field they used to park cars in was already filling up when the two friends arrived. Sage found a place as close as she could get to the actual sale since she knew they would be making many trips to the van.

"Are you ready? It looks like the sale is ten times bigger than the one they had in the fall."

"I am," Gabby said, hopping down from the van. "I'm looking for things for my house, too."

"There are a ton of people here already. If I hadn't had that argument with cranky old Mr. Peterson, we would have been here earlier, and I could be loading those two cradles in my van instead of those people," Sage said.

"Why on earth would you want baby cradles?"

"They make awesome rocking benches when converted."

"I can't see it, but then again, that's why you are the flipper," Gabby said.

"These mason jars will make a nice light fixture," Sage said, picking up the case of jars.

"Don't look now, but Cliff is heading our way," Gabby whispered.

Cliff Fulton was the twenty-eight-year-old son of the owners, Shirley and Pierce Fulton. He was six feet tall, well built from the farm work he did, and ruggedly handsome. It was known around the area that he had a crush on Sage, and he always made it a point to greet her when she came to the sale.

"Sage! Gabby! So good to see you here," Cliff said. "We have lots of great stuff to poke through."

"Hey, Cliff. How's things?" Gabby answered first.

"Things are going well. For the first time in almost six years, the farm is operating in the black. Mom and Dad are floating around here somewhere greeting everyone."

"I am so glad to hear things are going well for your family," Sage said, shifting the box of jars to her other arm.

"Let me take that," Cliff offered, reaching for the box. "I saved your same spot that you had last time if you want to collect your things and put them in a single space and load the van later."

"That would be awesome. Thank you," Sage said. "The one next to the barn?"

"Yes, it's all yours. We have twenty-five areas blocked off for buyers, and a couple of the farm hands are standing guard over the area to make sure things don't spring feet and walk away," he said, laughing. "I'll put these in your space so you can keep shopping."

"From the look of things, there is a lot of shopping to be done," Sage said, smiling.

"Give me a holler if you need any big pieces of furniture moved to your spot for you," he said, walking away.

"I will, and thanks again," Sage replied.

"I guess the rumors are true," Gabby said.

"Rumors?"

"Yes, ma'am. Cliff has the hots for you, and if you can't see it, then something is definitely wrong with you."

"He's nice to everyone," Sage said, blushing.

"You keep telling yourself that. I know you had a bad break-up with Perry, but Cliff is the whole package. Good looks, two college degrees, and a hard worker. And he is interested in you."

"I'm not ready for a new relationship yet."

"It's been over a year. Would you at least go have

a cup of coffee with him if he asked you?" Gabby replied.

"I'd think about it. Can we stop this dating talk and start shopping? I'm seeing a lot of things that I really want to get before someone else does."

Within three hours Sage had the biggest pile in the reserve area. Cliff ran a tally as the two women made trips to the van. The items bought for *This and That* had been set in a separate pile and were paid for with the credit card Sarah had given her daughter.

Gabby had found a few antiques to display in her salon and a fireplace set for her house. The van was full, but there were still a dozen pieces of furniture that would not fit. Cliff offered to load them in his truck and deliver the pieces to her shop the following day. He threw a blue tarp over the furniture and tied it down with twine promising to be there around two o'clock the following day.

"We'll stop at my mom's shop and drop off the things I bought for her. Then we can go unload the van at my workshop. I guess I can treat you to supper for all the work you have done today. Where do you want to eat?"

"I haven't been to the Cupston Diner for months. Can we eat there?"

"The diner it is," Sage said, pulling into her mother's shop.

"Mom?" Sage yelled, setting down a full box of smaller items on the counter. "Mom, where are you?"

Gabby noticed the back door to the shop was open, and the two friends exited the building looking for Sarah, hoping that the crazy man next door hadn't done anything to hurt her. The door to the new storage trailer was open. They walked up to the door and peered in. Sarah was moving furniture around and organizing the space.

"Mom what are you doing? The shop is wide open, and you're back here?"

"I was moving some of the larger pieces of furniture here to the trailer to empty the back of the shop. I want to rearrange the showcase area and set up the displays by rooms in the house instead of all the items just being tossed together willy-nilly."

"That sounds nice," Gabby said checking out a four-poster bed set against the wall of the trailer. "This is awesome."

"You already bought a beautiful antique sleigh bed that Sage refinished for you. You don't need another bed," Sarah said.

"I still have a second bedroom to outfit," Gabby

replied. "Although Rory said he might like to use that room as a home office after we get married."

"Better to wait, and I might already have a buyer for the bed," Sarah replied.

"We won't keep you. I put your credit card and receipt in the register drawer, and all the things we bought are on the counter and piled behind it. The van still has to be unloaded, and then we are going to the diner for supper if you want to join us."

"Thanks, but I'll have to pass this time. But I will see Gabby in the morning for my appointment," Sarah said, pushing a bureau to the back of the trailer.

"Okay, love you. And don't overdo it," Sage said.

"I won't. Love you more."

Five o'clock rolled around. The van contents had been emptied into the garage, and the women were on their way to the diner. It was Monday night, and the diner was busy, which was weird. Usually, Monday nights were slower than the weekend nights.

"Well, hello, strangers," Claire Marks, the owner of the diner, greeted the two friends. "Long time, no see."

"It has been a long time. Why is it so busy on a Monday night?" Sage asked.

"We are always busy the day of the farm sale. People tend to stop here and eat after the sale concludes. I just had a booth clear, so you are in luck, no waiting," she said, picking up a couple of menus.

They chattered with Claire as they walked toward the back of the diner when a shrill and irritating voice broke the peacefulness of the eatery. Everyone turned in the direction of the voice. Flora Peterson was clutching her fork and knife looking directly at Sage.

"We can't even go out to eat in peace without your family following us and causing problems," Flora screamed, slamming her utensils down on the wooden tabletop.

"What are you talking about, Flora?" Claire asked, bewildered at her customer's behavior.

"Her!" she said, glaring at Sage.

Claire turned to look at Sage who was furious at the way Flora was acting up in public.

"Really? I was walking by your table. How am I causing a problem for you, Flora?"

By now, most of the diners were watching the scene in front of them. Many of them were friends with Sage's mother and knew the problems the Petersons were causing her, and now it looked like they were doing the same thing to her daughter.

"You followed us here just to make us uncomfortable so we couldn't enjoy our meal," she accused the

young woman. "Just like your mother, a real troublemaker."

"For your information we just left the farm sale
and stopped here for dinner like many others who are
here eating. But had I known you were here, I would
have requested and waited for a seat in the patio room
because I would hate to waste a good meal by
throwing it up upon seeing you," Sage countered.

"Good one, girlfriend," Gabby whispered.

The room broke into fits of laughter which infuriated the complaining woman even more. Even Claire
had to stifle a laugh and turned away from the Petersons so they wouldn't see her face.

"You tell her, Sage!" someone yelled from behind
them.

"Well, I never! Come on, Ralph, we are leaving
right now. And if you think I am paying for this, this
food, as you call it, you are sadly mistaken. My
chickens eat better than this slop."

"That's pretty funny seeing as you don't even own
any chickens," Sage said loud enough for all to hear.
"If you don't want to pay your bill, I think the sheriff
should be called."

Again, the other customers broke out laughing.
Flora shoved Sage out of the way and hurried by her.
Ralph slid out of the bench seat and quietly issued a

warning to Sage on his way out. She took out her phone to call the sheriff.

"Let it go," Claire said, tapping Sage's cell phone. "They may think they got away with something today, but next time they come here to eat, they won't be allowed in and will be turned away each time after that."

"Classic," Gabby said.

"Do you still want to eat?" Claire asked.

"You bet we do. The atmosphere just got a lot more pleasant in here, and I'm starving. Besides, I owe my friend here a dinner for all her hard work today."

Two hours later, Sage dropped Gabby off at home and continued to her own house. She passed by her mother's shop which was in darkness, signaling her mother must have finished the display room and gone home for the evening. Tomorrow was her mother's day off, and Sage's turn to watch the store. Sleep came easily that night for Sage since they'd been out in the fresh air all day.

At eight o'clock, Sage was unlocking the doors to *This and That*. Before opening the store for business, she checked around to make sure it had stayed secure during the night. As she walked by the window in the back room, she saw a man leaving the Peterson house next door.

I wonder who that is.

Seeing nothing out of place, she put the money in the register drawer and flipped the sign on the door to open.

On Tuesdays, Sage cleaned the shop for her mom. She dusted all the doodads, washed the windows, and swept the floor from front to back. Then she would catalogue any new items that had arrived at the store and tag them for her mother to price them the next day.

The morning had been almost void of customers. Sage kept looking out the window to see if anyone was coming, but the parking lot out front remained empty. Checking her watch, she knew her mother would just be sitting in the beautician's chair to begin her scheduled appointment, and she didn't want to disturb her on her day off.

Sage was eating lunch when the bell on the door sounded. Mrs. Topps, her mom's best friend, walked up to the counter.

"I have a strange question," she said. "If you are open as usual, why is there a sign in front of the parking lot fence that says you are closed and gone out of business?"

"Excuse me?"

"There's a big sign out front. I thought it was kind of weird, so I figured I'd come in to check. Sarah never mentioned a thing to me about closing the shop."

"There's got to be some mistake," Sage said, coming out from behind the counter and heading for the door.

Mrs. Topps followed her outside and showed her where the sign was sitting. It was a big wooden A-frame that said exactly what she said it did. Sage looked up to see Mr. Peterson standing on his front porch smiling. The young woman knew instantly where the sign had come from and who put it there. He was purposely chasing away her mother's customers to put her out of business. She took pictures of the sign and called the sheriff's office.

"This wasn't here early this morning when I pulled into the parking lot," Sage said.

"I knew something wasn't right," her mom's friend said after listening to Sage's conversation with the sheriff's office. "This shop is Sarah's baby, and she would never close it."

Sheriff White pulled up in front of where the two women were standing. As he got out of the car, Ralph Peterson hurried into his house and slammed the door.

Sage explained what Peterson had done and that it had chased away her mother's customers for a good portion of the day. He left to go have a talk with the neighbor.

Sage took the wooden sign and threw it out back behind the trailer. She wanted Peterson to claim it if he wanted the wood back, thus admitting it was his in the first place. Walking back to the front of the store, she could hear loud yelling coming from inside the house next door. Minutes later, the sheriff exited with Ralph and Flora screaming at him as he left their front porch.

"I wish when they had moved, they moved to another state," the sheriff stated, frowning. "No, they had to stay in Cupston."

"You have dealt with these two before, haven't you?" Sage asked.

"Too many times to count. They don't believe in the law or rules, only their own."

"I hear they were a real handful when they lived on the other side of town," Sage said. "The Snows said their son, along with the whole neighborhood where they lived, had an awful time with them."

"They are not behaving any better here," Mrs. Topps declared, pursing her lips, and shaking her head.

"That's the truth. I was called out every day to the neighborhood to break up some kind of disturbance that always involved the Petersons. For the life of me, I could never figure out why they settled here. They have no family in the area. One day, they just showed up out of nowhere and bought the house on Concord Street."

"They are not fit to be living anywhere near other people," Sage said.

"I truly thought if they moved farther out into the country and away from an overcrowded neighborhood, there would be fewer problems. I never dreamed they would cause this much trouble for Sarah."

"So, what do we do about them?" Sage asked.

"Right now, nothing."

"So, they get to act however they want, and continue to cause trouble for my mother and her business?" Sage asked.

"I didn't say that. I gave Ralph Peterson a verbal warning. Next time…"

"What do you mean next time? We just have to wait for him to pull something else? What if he hurts my mother or tries to burn the place down? Then can we do something?"

"If you let me finish."

"Sorry," Sage replied.

"I gave him a verbal warning about trespassing on this property. And I told him that Claire was pressing charges against them for not paying their bill at the diner. They blamed the whole situation on you, but I had already talked to other witnesses that were there last night and got quite a different story than the one the Petersons tried to portray."

"I didn't do anything but walk by their booth on the way to mine," Sage said. "I didn't even look at them."

"I know, and it's in the report."

"So, we just continue on like nothing has happened?" Sage asked.

"I told the Petersons the next time they step foot on your mother's property, I will arrest them for trespassing. I am also going to suggest to Sarah to take out a restraining order."

"Yeah, we all know how well those things work, especially against someone like the Petersons."

"It's a step in the right direction in controlling the things that they can do," Sheriff White replied, heading for his cruiser. "And legally, that's all that can be done for now. Have a good rest of the day."

"You, too, Sheriff," Mrs. Topps said.

Sage stood there watching the sheriff drive away.

Ralph Peterson stepped out onto his front porch the minute he was gone and began his endless taunting with name calling and insults again. She held up her cell phone as if she was recording him again. He laughed at her.

"I don't think I have ever met such a rude person in my entire life," Mrs. Topps said.

"And my poor mother has to deal with him every day," Sage said. "I know you are meeting my mom later for bingo. Please don't mention what happened here today, Mrs. Topps. I will be at the shop first thing in the morning to tell her myself. I don't want her one day off to be ruined."

"I won't say a word. I promise. Be careful the rest of the day," Mrs. Topps said. "And please, we are all adults, call me Karen."

"I'll try," Sage said, smiling. "It's just I have called you Mrs. Topps since I was a little girl, and it might be hard to change my ways now."

"Either way, have a good night," she said, going out the door.

The afternoon business picked up once the sign had been removed. Many of the customers complained to Sage that some crazy man next door was yelling insults at them as they exited their cars to come into the shop. Several even told her that he had scared them, and they would not be back until the matter was addressed.

She called the sheriff to report that he was harassing the customers just so it would be on record. He promised to pay the Petersons another visit in the morning. Seven o'clock rolled around. Sage checked the trailer out back to make sure it was locked, cleaned out the register, and walked to her car. She watched Ralph Peterson in her rearview mirror, sitting on his front porch watching her as she left.

CHAPTER TWO

Sage wanted to arrive at the shop a little ahead of her mother. She had stopped for two coffees on her way there and also bought her mother a warm cinnamon bun which was her favorite thing to eat from the Coffee Café.

They sat at the counter drinking their morning coffee as Sage told her mother what had happened the previous day and that the sheriff would be arriving sometime in the morning to go talk to the Petersons again. She told her mother that she would stay at the shop until the sheriff arrived.

Open for business, Sarah was pricing the items that Sage had tagged the previous day while her daughter was attempting to make the display rooms a little homier looking. A doily here and a pillow there made the rooms more welcoming.

"It's kind of quiet around here, don't you think?" Sage asked her mother as she returned to the counter for more of her coffee.

"I agree. I wonder what Ralph is planning right now," Sarah replied. "Maybe we should go outside and take a look around."

The two women checked the parking lot to make sure no more signs had popped up where they shouldn't be. They walked the back perimeter of the property, and nothing had been touched, not even the stakes in the ground. The sign that Sage had thrown behind the trailer was still where she put it.

"Maybe they went away for the day," Sarah suggested as they returned to the shop through the back door. "It's pretty bad when peace and quiet make you more nervous than someone's crazy antics do."

"Anyone here?" a voice yelled from the front door.

"Gabby? What are you doing here?" Sage asked.

"I decided when I took on the three new hairdressers and enlarged my shop that I could take two days off instead of one. I talked to Rory last night about the second bedroom, and he said that we would need a second bedroom for visitors and maybe someday a nursery. He said he could build an addition off the back of the house to use as an office instead. So, I came to see if you heard from those other customers about the bed in the trailer."

"Persistent, aren't you?" Sarah asked, smiling. "As a matter of fact, I did hear from them yesterday afternoon, and they passed on the bed. If you want it, it's yours."

"Seriously? I definitely want it. Can I buy it today?"

"Why don't you take a look at it one more time to make sure you really want it. There are a few deep dings in it that Sage will have to fix for you. Here is the key to the padlock," Sarah said, taking a key off the holder behind the register counter.

"I'll be right back," she said, taking the key.

"When Gabby has her sights set on something, she never lets go of it," Sage said, chuckling. "Are the dings in the wood deep?"

Before Sarah could answer, a bloodcurdling scream sounded from outside.

"That was Gabby," Sage said, taking off in a dead run.

Sage exited the door first and saw her friend lying on the ground next to the door of the trailer. Fearing that the neighbors had set a boobytrap on the trailer door she ran to Gabby hoping for the best.

"Gabby! Are you okay? What happened?" Sage asked as Sarah joined them.

"I'll call an ambulance," Sarah said, taking out her cell phone.

"I don't need an ambulance. But I think you will need to call the police," Gabby stammered. "And maybe an ambulance for him."

"Him who?"

"The body that is wedged under the footboard of the four-poster bed. He didn't even move when I dropped the bed back down on him and ran."

"Stay here with Gabby, Mom," Sage said as she headed for the trailer door.

Sage stepped forward carefully so she wouldn't disturb anything. Two shod feet were sticking out from under the footboard. She lifted it just high enough to see that the person who was hidden underneath was Ralph Peterson.

"Mr. Peterson? Can you hear me?" Sage said, softly kicking his foot with hers.

No answer, and no movement.

Setting the bed down where it was originally when the body was found, Sage returned to her mother and Gabby.

"Have you called the sheriff yet?" Sage asked

"I was waiting to hear from you. Is there really a body inside the trailer?" Sarah asked.

"There is, and it's Mr. Peterson. I do believe he's dead. You'd better make that call now."

The dispatcher told the women to stay away from the crime scene area. While they waited, Sage noticed that Flora Peterson had come out onto the porch to watch.

"I'll be right back," Sage said.

Wanting to talk to the woman about the last time she saw the dead man, Flora met her at the edge of the yard and wouldn't let Sage take another step.

"You have been told to stay off our property. When Ralph gets home from his bowling tournament, you'll be sorry," she warned. "Now leave immediately!"

"When is he due home?"

"Any minute now. He spent the night in Lewiston, and if he didn't place in the money bracket, he will not be a pleasant person to deal with, especially toward you and your mother. Now, leave."

Two cruisers came screaming up the road and pulled into the shop parking lot. A few moments later, the coroner's van pulled in. Sage stood with Flora, watching her reaction, but there was none. Flora turned and walked calmly back to the porch. She continued to stare ahead blankly as the police entered the back yard and then the trailer. The sheriff stopped to talk to Gabby and Sarah and then headed across the yard toward Flora and Sage.

"I'm afraid I have some bad news for you, Flora. Ralph's body has been found in the trailer, and he is deceased. I'm very sorry," the sheriff said, taking off his hat in respect.

The woman didn't say a word. She looked from Sage to the sheriff, and back to Sage again. Her face hardened. She was clenching her fists, and her breathing sped up.

"You did this," she said, accusing Sage of the death. "You said the world would be better off if we were dead, and you went and did it, didn't you?"

"What's she talking about?" the sheriff asked, looking at Sage.

"I may have made that comment in front of some people outside the shop, but I sure didn't have anything to do with killing Ralph. I was mad when I said what I did, but I didn't mean it literally."

"Flora, when is the last time you saw him?"

"Last night when he left for his bowling tournament."

"And what time was that?"

"I don't know. Right after supper, so it was probably just after six o'clock."

"I don't think so. I closed the shop a little after seven, and Ralph was sitting on the porch watching me when I drove away," Sage said, correcting her time frame.

"I don't know. It could have been seven, I'm so confused right now," Flora said, wringing her hands. "Are you sure it was Ralph that you found?"

"I'm sure. I need you to come down to the station to answer some questions. Can you do that?"

"I can, but the one you should be questioning is standing right next to you."

"We will be speaking with everyone involved," the sheriff replied. "Will you take a walk to the trailer with me and identify the body?"

Flora looked horrified at the suggestion.

"Do I have to?" she squeaked out in a pitchy voice.

"It has to be done. You can do it here or down at the coroner's office. I will leave the choice up to you," the sheriff said.

"Let's get this over with. Show me where he is," she said, stepping down off the porch and strutting toward the trailer where everyone was gathered.

"Did you notice she didn't shed a tear?" Sage

asked the sheriff in a whisper as they followed behind her.

"I did, but people react differently to death."

Flora stopped a few feet away from Sarah. The two women stared at each other waiting for the other one to speak first.

"I hope you and your daughter are happy with yourselves. Ralph is gone, and I won't be sticking around here in this little geedunk town. You got what you wanted," Flora said.

"I never wanted anything like this to happen. I just wanted to be left alone," Sarah replied.

"All right, Flora. Come this way please," the sheriff said, steering her toward the trailer door and away from Sarah.

The two disappeared inside, returning a few seconds later. Flora was visibly shaken, and the sheriff offered to walk her back to her house. She refused his offer and said she would meet him at the station.

"I never thought I would see the day…" she mumbled as she walked away.

"I think she's in shock. I don't think it's a good idea for her to be driving," Gabby said. "She doesn't like you two very well, but maybe she would accept a ride from me to the police station."

"You can try, but I don't think she'll accept your help either," Sage replied.

Gabby ran after Flora to offer to drive her to the station, but the woman refused any help. Everyone watched as she started to wave her hands in the air like a mad woman and scream at Gabby that she didn't need help from the friend of a killer. The young woman walked away and back to the group near the trailer.

"You tried. Don't feel bad," the sheriff said to Gabby.

"I don't, it was just weird, that's all."

"What was weird?" Sage asked.

"Flora was. She said she would drive herself since she wouldn't be returning to the house and needed to drive her own vehicle."

"I wonder if it has anything to do with the guy that left her house early yesterday morning," Sage pondered out loud. "Maybe she was having an affair behind Ralph's back."

"What guy?" the sheriff asked.

"I don't know who he was. I had never seen him before yesterday morning. But he came out of the Peterson house and hurried up the street without looking back."

"I'm glad you said something so I can question

Flora about him when she arrives at the station. What did he look like?"

"Maybe Flora's age. Dark hair, tall and thin. He was in a pin-striped suit and carried a briefcase," Sage replied.

"I've never seen anyone around like that," Sarah said.

"I'll find out who he was," the sheriff said. "Meanwhile, please stay out of the trailer for now until I tell you it's okay to go back inside. It is a murder scene, and I'm sure Flora will be insisting that one of you be charged for the death. I don't want it said you had access to the evidence inside."

"I'll even give you the keys to the door," Sarah said, holding out a key ring.

"And just so you know, I really don't want the bed anymore, thank you. I couldn't crawl into it and sleep peacefully knowing that someone dead had been hidden underneath it," Gabby said to Sarah.

"I understand perfectly," Sarah said, patting Gabby's hand.

The body was wheeled away on a gurney, and yellow police tape was hung around the trailer. The group watched as Flora placed three suitcases in the back of her SUV and slammed it closed.

"If I didn't know better, I would say Flora is going on the run," Sarah said.

"I think I'll follow her to the station," the sheriff said. "She might think twice about it if I am right behind her."

"Good luck," Sarah said.

The coroner locked the trailer using the keys the sheriff handed off to him. He reminded the women to stay clear and left with the body.

Word had circulated around town that Ralph Peterson was dead, and locals were coming to the shop to see if it was true. The parking lot was filling up, along with the shop. Many of the people who were showing up were people that had lived in the neighborhood with the Petersons before they moved in next to Sarah.

"Is it true? Is Ralph dead?" Edna Collins, the self-proclaimed town historian, asked Sarah.

"He is."

"And they found him in your trailer?"

"Yes, they did, Edna. Are you insinuating something?" Sarah asked the town busybody. "If you are, just come right out and ask whatever it is you are thinking but not saying."

"Well, did you? Did you pick off that old goat?"

"Seriously, Edna? Do you really think my mother

has it in her to kill anybody? And if she did, or anybody did for that fact, do you think they would admit to murdering someone?"

"I can see why Ralph had problems with the two of you," she answered in a huff.

"Why Ralph had problems with them? You can't be serious, Edna," Mrs. Topps said, walking up to the counter. "Ralph had problems with any person he lived nearby. He was the troublemaker."

"I never had any problems with the man."

"No, because he had to stay on your good side because you were the one who filed all his complaints with the town. I think that right there should tell you what kind of person he was."

"So, who killed him then?" Edna asked.

"We don't know. The sheriff is working on it," Sarah replied.

"Was the trailer locked last night?"

"Yes, it was, Edna."

"So, how did someone get the body in there? It would be obvious to anyone with a brain that you would have to have a key to dump the body. Well, who had keys?"

"There was only one key to the padlock on the door, and it was hanging on the key rack behind the register," Sage answered. "And it was there this morning when my mom gave the key to Gabby to go look at a bed that was being stored out there."

"That should tell you all you need to know about who killed Ralph Peterson," Edna said loudly. "The only key, and who had possession of it, Sarah?"

"Let's talk about using your brain, Edna. Do you think if my mom killed him and hid him in the trailer, she would just hand over a key for someone to go in there and find him?"

"I guess not. But that doesn't answer the question of how the body got in there in the first place," Edna replied.

"I'm sure the sheriff will figure it out," Sarah said. "Can we change the subject now, please?"

"I'm keeping my eye on you, Sarah, both you and your daughter. And I will be checking in with the sheriff periodically. We can't have killers running around loose in the town. It's time to go back to work."

"You do that, Edna," Sarah replied, trying to hold her temper.

"Don't let the door hit you in the backside on your way out," someone yelled from the display room.

"That woman is so aggravating. She thinks just because her ancestors settled this town hundreds of years ago that she has a say in everything that happens in Cupston," Karen Topps said. "It would figure that she would be friends with Ralph Peterson. Two of a kind."

"As much of a pain as Edna is, she did bring up a good point. How did the body get in the trailer when the only key to the padlock was locked in the shop?" Sarah said.

"Mom, anyone can pick those padlocks. They're sold at any hardware store out there."

"I wouldn't even have had a padlock on there if it wasn't for Ralph. The other storage units don't have locks on them, just that one because it was so close to his property. I've never needed to lock anything up in this town. I haven't set the alarm system in the shop for over twenty years."

"I wouldn't say that too loudly," Gabby said. "There's quite a few strangers milling about in the shop."

"Point taken," Sarah replied.

"I guess I'll go do my weekly food shopping since I'm going home without the bed," Gabby said. "I'll stop at the police station on the way and fill out my report. I can truthfully say that I never ever thought in this lifetime I would find a dead body. Now, Sage, yes, I would expect that to happen to you."

"Excuse me," Sarah said, answering her ringing cell phone.

"I need to get home and get some work done," Sage said, grabbing her car keys from behind the counter. "Talk to you later, Mom."

"Sage!" her mother yelled as she was about to get in the car. "Can you come here a minute?"

"What's up, Mom?" she asked returning to the shop.

"That was Sheriff White. He wants me to come down to the station right now to give my statement. Flora is throwing quite a tantrum that she is being held there and I am not. Do you mind staying at the shop a little while longer while I run down there and file my report?"

"Good thing I am my own boss," Sage said, smiling. "I'll stay."

"I'll get back as quick as I can," Sarah promised.

The shop stayed busy as more people came to see the crime scene. There hadn't been a murder in Cupston in over twenty years. Crime, yes, but murder, no. After they viewed the yellow police tape and found out they couldn't go into the trailer, they came in to shop instead. Sage pretty much was stuck behind the register all afternoon. Sarah returned right before five and after the rush had concluded.

"I'm sorry it took so long. I have never answered so many questions in my life. Everything I said was the complete opposite of what Flora said. It seems busybody Edna went to the station prior to me getting there and offered her viewpoint regarding the only key hanging in the shop, and Flora overheard the conversation. I guess I am on the top of the suspect list now."

"Sheriff White knows you didn't do it."

"I'm not so sure," Sarah said, throwing her purse under the counter.

"Come on, Mom. He knows all the problems you have had with the Petersons, and you have followed the letter of the law in all those dealings."

"Yes, I have. Let Edna run her mouth. She'll look like the fool when they find the real killer," Sarah replied.

"Besides, you are way too smart to kill someone and leave the body on your own property. You would have at least hidden him out in the woods," her daughter said, trying to make her mom smile.

"Not funny, Sage. They are seriously thinking I had something to do with Ralph Peterson's death, and Edna blabbing about the key all over town isn't going to help my situation."

"I'm sorry. Quick question before I leave. Do you

want to go with me and Gabby to help clean out Mrs. Snow's aunt's house? I know the shop is usually open that day, so if you want me to grab some things for you, I will."

"I could use a restock on some smaller items. You know, doodads, figurines, jewelry, and that kind of stuff. Kitchen things tend to move fast, but no more pots and pans. I have half a trailer of those out back."

"Okay. I figured I would ask in case I don't see you in the next couple of days. I have lots of new projects to start and will be pretty much glued to my workshop. Love you and don't worry. Sheriff White will catch whoever killed Ralph, and Edna will have to eat crow in front of all of Cupston," Sage said heading for the front door.

Sage started her car and happened to glance over at the Peterson house. Flora's SUV was not there. A movement in the second-floor window caught her attention. Someone was in the house, and it wasn't Ralph or Flora. She shut off her car and hurried over to find out who it was.

Standing on the front porch she put her ear to the front door to listen. Someone was definitely inside, and it sounded like they were moving furniture around.

"Who's in there?" she yelled, banging on the front door.

The noise stopped with the first bang on the door.

"I know you're in there. I saw you in the second-floor window. You'd better come to the door, or I will call the sheriff," Sage threatened.

No one came to the door, and the noises didn't resume. Sage walked around to the back of the house just in time to hear a car motor start up farther up the street. Whoever had been inside escaped through the back door. She checked the back door, and it was locked up tight.

Cutting across the back yard, she climbed into her car again, this time to see Flora pull in next door. She ran to the neighbor's house for a second time and stopped Flora before she went into the house.

"Flora! Hold up a second," she yelled as the woman unlocked the door.

"What do you want now? It's been an extremely long day."

"Someone was in your house and ran away when I checked on them," Sage said, watching for a reaction. "Should someone have been in there with you gone?"

"No … are you sure you saw someone? Could you tell who it was?"

"I couldn't tell you who it was. They ran out the

back door before I could get close enough to identify them. Does anyone else have a key to the house? Could you be in danger, too?"

"No one else has a key," she whispered.

"Do you want me to go in the house with you and see if we can figure out how they entered your house? You need to feel safe being by yourself now."

"Why are you being so nice to me? Do you think I will change my mind that either you or your mother is guilty of killing Ralph?"

"You can think what you want, Flora. I just don't want the same thing to happen to you that happened to Ralph."

"I can look out for myself, thank you very much."

"Fine, have a nice night," Sage said, stepping down off the porch.

As she walked to her car, she kept glancing over her shoulder watching Flora. The woman hadn't moved off the front porch. She was just standing there looking at the door.

I do believe she is afraid to go into her own house.

"Flora, are you okay?" Sage yelled. "Do you want me to come back?"

The distraught woman turned and shook her head yes.

"Stay behind me," Sage said as she opened the door.

The two women entered the house and were shocked at what was displayed in front of them. The house had been ransacked and was a mess.

"Don't touch anything," Sage instructed. "I'm going to call the sheriff."

Flora sat down on the stairs that led to the second floor and started to weep. Sage strolled around the first floor looking for an entrance way that would tell them how the intruder gained access to the house. She found a small window over the kitchen sink that was open and figured that this must have been the point of entry.

"Hello," the sheriff yelled from the front door.

"Come in," Flora replied from the stairs.

"I think whoever did this came in through the kitchen window above the sink," Sage said, returning to the front door. "You might want to start looking for fingerprints there."

"I have a team on the way. Flora, are you okay?" the sheriff inquired, watching her crying with her face buried in her hands.

"She wasn't home, thank goodness," Sage replied.

"Flora, can you think of anyone that would have done this to your home and why?"

"No, I can't."

"What about the man who I saw leaving your house the other morning?" Sage asked.

Flora stopped crying and stared at Sage.

"You saw Paul leaving? But we were so careful," Flora stammered.

"Who is Paul?' the sheriff asked.

"He's my attorney," Flora replied.

"Your attorney or you and Ralph's attorney?"

"My attorney. Ralph didn't know I had retained Paul, or he would have…" Her voice trailed off.

"He would have what, Flora?" Sage asked.

"It doesn't really matter now, does it? Ralph is gone," she replied.

"Do you have any idea who would have done this to your house or why?" the sheriff asked.

"I can think of lots of people who hated Ralph, but what they were looking for, I don't know," she replied, sighing heavily.

"What did Ralph do before he retired?" Sage asked.

"Do I have to answer all these questions again?" Flora asked the sheriff. "I told you all I know already at the station."

"No, you don't. I'm sure Sage is just trying to help," he replied. "The officers are here to fingerprint the house. Do you want to stay where you are, or do you want to sit on the porch, Flora?"

"I'll be out on the porch," she answered, standing up and heading out the front door.

"Sage! Flora! Are you okay?" Sarah yelled, running across the front lawn.

"We're fine, Mom. It seems someone broke into Flora's house while you were both at the police station," Sage answered.

"You were at the police station today?" Flora asked.

"I was there all afternoon, just like you," Sarah replied.

"Then it couldn't have been you in the house."

"No, it wasn't," Sarah confirmed. "Why would you think it was me?"

"I don't know. Ralph always told me you were an evil person who was trying to make us move. I thought you were trying to scare me into leaving by doing this."

"I never once said I wanted you to move. I just wanted Ralph to leave me alone and let me run my shop in peace," Sarah answered.

"He could be quite cantankerous when he wanted to be," Flora admitted, sitting down on the porch swing. "I'm just glad it's over."

"What's over?" Sage asked.

"Never mind, it's not important. There will be no more problems from me concerning your shop, Sarah."

"That's good to know. You could come over and visit the shop once in a while and maybe have a cup of tea," Sarah suggested.

"That would be nice. Ralph never let me leave the house. It would be nice to have a friend, a female friend to chat with. I'm sorry I accused you of murdering Ralph. I guess his lousy attitude wore off on me more than I thought after living with him all these years."

"How long have you been married?" Sage asked.

"Does it matter? He's gone, and I can live my own life now. I'm not really as bad a person as everyone thinks I am. If you'll excuse me, I want to see if the sheriff has found anything in the house," Flora said, standing up, signaling it was time for the women to leave.

"Call me if you need anything. I'm only five minutes up the road," Sarah said as they were leaving.

"That was weird," Sage said as they walked back to the shop. "Flora did a complete turnaround toward you."

"I don't know. Maybe she had to act like she did

when she was around Ralph. He did seem pretty domineering. I'll give her a second chance. Maybe you should, too."

"I'll think about it. But then again, maybe Flora is the killer, and she did it to get out from under her husband's thumb. Maybe she needs you as an ally instead of an enemy now."

"You've read too many mystery novels," Sarah said, laughing. "But I will be careful when she's around."

"Let me know if you change your mind about going on Saturday. Gabby is going into work at noon instead of nine so she can go," Sage said, sliding into the front seat of her car for the third time.

"I'll let you know by Friday night," her mother promised, closing the car door and waving goodbye before disappearing inside.

The next several days, Sage worked diligently in her shop, starting new projects and rearranging to make room for the items when the house was cleaned out on Saturday. The four chairs she had picked up from the trash pile on the side of the road were coming along nicely. The scratched brown wooden frames had been sanded and had been repainted a flat black. The seat cushions had been reupholstered with a black, white, and gray geometric material and went perfectly with the black paint.

I can sell these for two hundred for the set. Not a bad profit since they were free to begin with. I think I'll work on the mason jar light fixture next.

Hanging an old ox yoke that was dated to the early 1900s up above her work bench, she set to work wiring the top of the wood so the electrical cords would not be noticeable from below when it hung above someone's table. She drilled four evenly spaced holes through the yoke to feed the wires through where the mason jars would hang. Drilling holes in the metal tops of the jars, she fed the wires through and secured the sockets and clear glass bulbs inside the jars; the chandelier lit up.

"I think Gabby is going to want this, too," Sage said, stepping back and admiring the dancing lights. "Let me see. The yoke cost me ten dollars, the jars five dollars. The wiring and sockets were all parts from other projects. I think one twenty-five is a good starting price in Mom's shop."

Sage's stomach started growling. She had worked through lunch and had only had a cup of coffee earlier in the day. Deciding to go to the diner for a quick bite of supper, she locked up her shop after laying out her projects for the following day.

It was payday for a lot of the people that worked in the area. The diner was busy, so Sage grabbed a seat at the counter. She picked up a menu after glancing over the specials board. Perusing the menu, she heard a familiar voice behind her mention her name. She turned to see Edna and several other women sitting at a table a few feet away.

"Don't you find it truly amazing that someone can be involved in a murder and yet walk around free? I just don't understand how the law works nowadays," Edna said loudly, staring directly at Sage.

The other women seated at the table with her whispered among themselves but kept glancing in Sage's direction. Sage closed the menu she was reading and calmly got up from her stool. She walked to the obnoxious woman's table and leaned on it, her hands right next to Edna's plate.

"Do you have something you would like to say directly to my face, Edna?"

"How do you know I was talking about you? Guilty conscience?"

"Oh, I know. You have run your mouth all over town to anyone who would listen about the key in my mom's shop. So, who else that's eating in here tonight would you be centering your gossip and ill-thought-out opinions on besides me?" Sage asked, looking around the diner.

"Really? My opinions are well thought out, and if there is only one key to the trailer, then what other conclusion could one come to?"

"Did you ever stop to think that those dime-a-dozen padlocks are easily picked, and it could have been anybody? Maybe it could have been you, Edna."

The women around the table snickered, and that infuriated Edna. She glared at them, and they stopped immediately, but she couldn't silence the rest of the chuckling that was going on around the diner.

"Why would I kill Ralph Peterson? He was always pleasant to me, and unlike you and your mother, I never had a problem with him," Edna stated.

"We all know about your good rapport with Ralph at the town hall. I do believe that every complaint he ever registered with the town had your signature on the bottom of it. Correct me if I'm not right, please," Sage countered.

"That's my job," she said through gritted teeth.

"It was your job to file baseless complaints? How many were dismissed? How many problems did you cause for the locals of this town filing those complaints? You also made a lot of people angry, and it's a wonder you're not in the trailer right alongside Ralph," Sage said.

"Sometimes rich people deserve what they get," Edna replied, her eyes narrowing. "Are you threatening me?"

"No, just my ill-thought-out opinion. Have a nice night," Sage said, walking back to her stool.

"Are you ever going to come in here and eat without starting a ruckus?" Claire, the owner, asked Sage as she sat down.

"I hope so," Sage said.

"It's okay. Once in a while, Edna needs to be put in her place. I just hope she doesn't end up dead next after what you said."

"I was only trying to prove a point about people's personal opinions. I might have gone a little overboard. Maybe I should apologize to Edna."

"You will do no such thing. Let her stew in what you said to her," Claire said, pouring a glass of water for Sage. "Do you know what you want to order?"

Sage ordered the fried shrimp basket with French fries, coleslaw, and extra drawn butter. An iced tea with lemon finished off her order. Edna and her cronies left shortly after she ordered, and Sage was able to eat in peace the rest of the time she was there.

Arriving home shortly after seven, she pulled her

car up to the workshop and put on the high beams. Cliff Fulton had been there while she was at the diner and dropped off the furniture from the farm sale. He had called on Tuesday afternoon to tell her the delivery would be delayed and wasn't sure when he would get the items delivered, but it would be sometime during the week. Leaving the car lights on so she could see, she moved the pile into her workshop. They were forecasting rain over night, so she felt better getting the items inside and not leaving them under the blue tarp outside. Glancing around, she realized she didn't have a lot of extra room for anything she had picked up on Saturday.

I may have to do what my Mom did and get a storage trailer for behind my garage. Luckily, no one lives close enough that it would be an eyesore for them.

She locked the door and turned around to see Cliff pulling up the driveway.

"I was hoping I would get here in time to help you move your stuff inside, but you beat me to it," he said, leaning out the window, smiling.

"I have to stay ahead of the rain," she replied. "Thanks for delivering it for me."

"No problem. I was wondering…"

Sage stood there waiting for him to finish his

sentence, even though she had an idea of what he was going to say. He took a deep breath and started again.

"I was wondering if you would like to go to dinner with me on Saturday night?"

"I would like that, but I'll have to let you know what time I get home. I'm picking a house over in Moosehead on Saturday. Mrs. Snow's aunt died, and they're cleaning out her house so it can be sold. We're leaving early to be there at eight in the morning, so I should be home by midafternoon."

"Great. I'll give you my cell number in case you run into any problems."

Sage entered his number into her phone, and they said their goodbyes. The first thing she did once inside the house was text Gabby to tell her she had a date on Saturday night. Her friend responded with 'I told you so' and signed off to go finish eating her supper.

The next morning, Sage loaded the finished chairs and light fixture into her van to bring them to her mother's shop. Before she left, she stripped the headboard and footboard down to the original wood and set them in front of her workbench to work on when she returned. She would cut the footboard in half and connect them to the headboard to create a hall bench with a storage area under the seat.

Quite a sight greeted Sage as she pulled into the parking lot at *This and That*. Her mother and Flora Peterson were sitting out front drinking sweet tea. They were laughing, and it was clear that they were comfortable spending time together. Sage exited her van and joined them.

"And to what do I owe this visit?" Sarah asked her daughter.

"Delivery," Sage answered. "Hello, Flora."

"Hello, Sage. Your mother and I were just chatting about you."

"Nothing bad I hope," Sage replied, eyeing Flora suspiciously.

"I see what you mean," Flora said to Sarah. "No nothing bad."

"Yes, that's my daughter. She doesn't trust anybody," Sarah said, smiling. "We were just discussing Flora's future."

"And that would be?" Sage asked.

"I have decided to stay put here in Cupston. Now that Ralph is gone, I don't have to hate and avoid people the way he did. I have found your mother to be quite a pleasant person and nothing like Ralph tried to convince me she was."

"I guess that's a good thing. Doesn't it bother you that the police still haven't found Ralph's killer?

Aren't you the least little bit afraid you might be next if you stay here?" Sage asked.

"Sage, really?" Sarah said, frowning.

"It's okay. I am afraid, and that is why my attorney is arranging for an alarm system to be installed in my house."

"Did you ever find out if anything was missing from your house after the break-in?" Sage asked, still not liking the neighbor's three-sixty towards her mother.

"There wasn't anything of value missing. The weird thing was most of the items that disappeared were Ralph's personal things, like financial paper-work, books, and jewelry. Nothing of mine was taken. My attorney did advise me to close all our joint accounts and charge cards just to be on the safe side."

"Well, be careful," Sage advised her. "Mom, I'm going to put the new items behind the counter. Wait until you see how the chairs came out. I will put the invoice and suggested prices in the register drawer. You can decide if you agree with them."

"Maybe you can come to my house and see if you want any of the things I am tossing out. I am redoing the whole house with Ralph's life insurance money. He was such a dreary person, and I want my house to be bright and homey," Flora stated.

"If you don't mind me asking, if your life was so unpleasant being married to him, why did you stay with him?" Sage asked.

"I don't think that is any of your business, Sage," Sarah jumped in.

"People do things for different reasons that other people might not understand. Let's leave it at that," Flora replied.

"I guess."

Sage emptied her van and returned to the two women still sitting outside.

"Have you decided if you're going to Moosehead tomorrow?" Sage asked her mother.

"I'm going to have to pass. I have four deliveries arriving tomorrow that I need to sign for. Can you pick up some stuff for me that you think might sell in the shop?"

"I can do that. I do have a date Saturday night—" Sage started to say.

"You have a date? With whom?" Sarah inquired, jumping up, and hugging her daughter.

"Jeez, Mom. Calm down. It's just a supper date with Cliff Fulton."

"I knew it. I knew you two would eventually get together. He's liked you for quite a while. I'm so glad you are finally moving past your bad relationship with Perry."

"As I was going to say, if I pick up stuff for you, I'll deliver it on Tuesday when I come watch the shop on your day off. Is that okay?"

"That's fine. That will give me something to work on Wednesday, which is the slowest day of the week," her mom replied.

"Great! Have a good day. I'm off to finish the hall bench and two end tables that I'm refinishing. I was looking around while I was inside. Do you have anywhere that I can display a drop-down desk that I converted into a nice bar? It's a bigger piece than I normally do, but it came out so beautiful. I would like to get three hundred for it."

"I'll make room near the front door. Bring it with you on Tuesday."

"Okay. I'll probably talk to you on Wednesday," Sage said, heading for her van. "Bye, Flora."

"Have a good day."

Sage sat in her van watching the two women who had returned to their conversing. There was something not right about Flora, but she couldn't put her finger on what it was … yet. A person doesn't change that fast unless it is for a very good reason. A reason that Sage would dig for until she found out what it was.

The rest of the afternoon was spent working in her shop. She finally quit and went into her house to grab some supper before going to bed early. While she ate, she texted Gabby to tell her she would be there at seven in the morning to pick her up for their trip to Moosehead. Her friend promised that she would have a thermos of coffee and some homemade blueberry muffins for the trip. Sage was in bed by ten.

CHAPTER THREE

The van was totally empty, and the rattling from the back area was extremely loud. Sage decided when she arrived at Gabby's she would spread out some of the furniture pads that she had brought with her to somewhat muffle the noise for the long trip.

Gabby was sitting on her front steps when Sage arrived. Rory, her fiancé, was sitting with her, enjoying a cup of coffee before heading off to work. He helped Sage spread out the pads in the van and then reminded Gabby to look for any old tools for his office or fishing poles to add to his collection. She promised to look for both and gave him a kiss goodbye. The women climbed into the van and set off for Moosehead.

As they drove, they chatted happily, covering

many different subjects. Gabby couldn't resist teasing her friend about the dinner invitation she received from Cliff to which Sage insisted it was just two friends going out to eat and nothing more. The conversation turned more serious when Sage told her friend about the way Flora had changed overnight and how she'd latched on to her mother. Gabby was suspicious of Flora's intentions as well.

They pulled into 57 Honeysuckle Lane. A large commercial dumpster was in the driveway with its back open. The two friends hopped down from their seats and were greeted by Mrs. Snow in the front yard.

"The family has spent the last week taking the items they wanted from the house. Anything that is left is up for grabs, so help yourself or it will end up in the dumpster over there. Sarah couldn't make it?" Mrs. Snow asked.

"Unfortunately, she had too many deliveries today that she had to be at the shop to accept. Is it okay if I grab some items for her since she couldn't make it?"

"Take whatever you think Sarah can sell and whatever you can use for your flipping. Gabby, make sure you take anything for your house that you want."

"This is so awesome. We don't know how to thank you for including us in this," Sage said.

"Just make sure you cram that van full," Mrs. Snow said. "If you have any questions, I'll be floating around somewhere, so just holler."

"This is so awesome," Sage said as they walked through the front door. "Look at all the stuff that's left. I can't believe the family didn't take some of these pieces."

"Shall we walk through each room together or go our separate ways?" Gabby asked.

"Let's do this together. It will be more fun."

They started in the living room.

Almost anything that was in decent shape was transferred to the van. Lamps, knickknacks, and all the remaining furniture except for the large couch was taken.

"Check these out," Sage said, going through the bookcase. "These are all yearbooks from the Moosehead and Cupston high schools that are right around when my mom graduated. I bet she would love these for her shop. And these old books are first editions, a lot of them signed. I don't think Mrs. Snow knows the value of these signed books. I need to tell her before I claim them."

After just the living room and kitchen, the van was almost half-full.

"We need to be a little more selective as we move on," Sage said.

In the small den, Sage found another desk that she could transform into a bar. Even though the lamps were modern-day purchases, Sage took them to cannibalize them for parts. Two wooden bookcases were also loaded in the van.

In the cellar, Gabby found some old tools which she claimed for Rory, and she put them in the van in the space under where her feet would be in the front seat. There were no fishing poles since the aunt hadn't gone fishing after her husband died and she'd gotten rid of all his outdoor items. Some older headboards and footboards were piled in the corner which Sage immediately took.

Six old, large fire extinguishers went next that could be transformed into industrial-style lamps. A wooden box was filled to the top with wire, screws, nails and other parts and pieces. A box of gold heater grates was also scooped up. A pile of old wooden apple crates and three old barn doors were taken out to the van.

"Sage! Gabby! Are you hungry?" Mrs. Snow yelled down the cellar stairs. "We have pizza and soda up here."

Sage looked at her watch. It was already one

o'clock, and they hadn't even hit the second floor yet. They carried up the last load from the cellar, washed their hands, and joined the Snows for lunch. While they ate, Sage told them about the books she'd found and how they were signed first editions. Mrs. Snow insisted she give them to her mother to put in her shop since she had no room for anything else at her house.

She also told Sage that she had her husband put a box in her van full of handmade linens and doilies that her aunt had made to go in Sarah's shop along with some quilts that were made back in the 1940s.

"Gabby, I know you were looking for a bed. In the spare bedroom is a beautiful four-poster-bed that was my mother's when she was a young girl. I would love for you to take it. You can get a new mattress and box spring for it."

"Thank you so much," Gabby said, wiping her hands on her napkin. "I can't wait to go look at it."

"If she doesn't take it, I will," Sage said. "Gabby, are you ready to start upstairs?"

"Let's go! This is so much fun," Gabby said, smiling at Mrs. Snow. "Thank you for lunch."

"Yes, thank you. We've been so busy we didn't realize how hungry we were."

"I'm so glad you are enjoying yourself and finding so many things you can use. It breaks my heart to throw things away, but I have no room after I took what I absolutely wanted to have to remind me of my aunt."

Entering the first bedroom, Gabby fell in love with the bed. They worked together to take it apart and slid it into the side of the van after wrapping it up in a furniture pad.

"I hate to ask, but do you think we can fit the small matching dresser into the van? I would love to keep the two pieces together," Gabby asked.

"Let's bring it downstairs and rearrange the van to make sure it fits," Sage replied.

"You're the best," Gabby said, hugging her friend.

After the dresser was tucked safely in the van, they returned to the second floor and went room to room loading boxes that had been left around for that purpose. Costume jewelry, purses, and fancy hats for her mother's shop were loaded into the smaller spaces between the bigger pieces in order to avoid wasting an inch of space.

As much as Sage wanted to take the master bedroom furniture, she passed on it to fit multiple smaller pieces of furniture into what space was left in the van. They packed all the remaining figurines, bird statues, and the teacup collection that had been lovingly displayed in the aunt's bedroom.

"I can't believe no one in the family wanted these things," Gabby said, closing up a box.

"I know, I don't understand it either, but today the younger kids are a throwaway society and don't want material things that belonged to family members," Mrs. Snow said from the doorway.

"I wish I had brought two vans," Gabby said. "Your aunt's possessions are awesome. I would really have liked to have taken that master bedroom suite for my own bedroom. Older furniture has so much more character than the newer modern stuff."

"I'll tell you what. We are going to be here for the next three or four days cleaning the house out. If you can promise to come back tomorrow, I can have you put whatever you couldn't fit in the van in one room, and I will leave it for you to come back and get it."

"Really? That would be wonderful. I really wanted the matching hutches that are downstairs besides the bedroom suite. If we pile things in the small den, I'll come back and get them tomorrow. Gabby, that would mean you could get the triple dresser to the bedroom set that we couldn't fit in the van," Sage said.

"I would much rather you take the things than throw them out," Mrs. Snow replied. "Mr. Snow and I have to leave for an hour or so. When you are done in the den, just slam the front door closed when you leave, making sure it is locked. We will see you tomorrow I guess."

"Thank you again. This has been the best day ever," Sage said.

"I can't believe she's letting us come back. That means I'll have the full suite in my spare bedroom. And now we can grab some of the items we were hesitant about taking because of space issues in the van," Gabby said. "Good thing the salon is closed on Sundays, and I don't have to move around anymore appointments for my clients."

"Let's get to work," Sage said, picking up a box to move to the den. "This has turned out to be an amazing day."

"And you haven't even gone on your date yet," Gabby added.

Sage threw her friend the old side-eye that she did when she wasn't going to argue with her and just accept what she had said. Gabby had been trying to play matchmaker ever since Sage ended her five-year relationship with Perry Fuller. She caught him dating someone else on the side, and the experience had left a sour taste in her mouth for dating and men.

Sage had been quite happy being single and not having to answer to anyone but herself, and occasionally her mother. Deep down, she still didn't know why she said yes to Cliff and going to dinner, but she was kind of glad she did. Although she would never admit that tidbit to Gabby or her mother.

By four o'clock, the small den was full, and the two friends had finished going through the entire house a second time. They closed the front door, making sure it was securely locked and headed for home with a fully loaded van. Just as they pulled up in front of Sage's workshop, Cliff called to check in on their progress. Figuring in the time to unload the van and to bring Gabby home, Sage told him she would be ready by six thirty.

As they emptied the van, they made two piles in the workshop; one for Sage's items and one for the things that would be moved to *This and That*. Gabby's furniture and boxes were returned to the van, and Sage took her friend home. Rory was there to help unload, which made things a little easier having a guy around to move the heavy stuff.

Back home again, Sage took a quick shower and dressed in a flowy, cotton midi-skirt and summer sweater. Not knowing where they were going to eat made it hard to figure out how to dress. Plus, Sage hadn't been out on a date for over a year and wasn't sure what to wear just for that reason alone. A skirt and pretty gold sandals would be pretty much accepted anywhere they went.

She was locking up the workshop when Cliff's truck pulled into the driveway. He hopped down out of the truck and headed her way.

"How did today go?" he asked.

"You tell me," she replied, removing the padlock from the door.

He stuck his head in, looked around, and let out a long whistle.

"You cleaned up today."

"The best part is I'm going back tomorrow to fill the van again. Mrs. Snow gave me another day to come back and grab some more stuff. Anything I don't take is going into a dumpster, and she said she would rather see my mom and I have it verses the dump."

"The Snows are such nice people. They have been friends with my parents for many years, ever since I can remember. No one knows this, but it was the Snows that loaned my parents money years ago so they wouldn't lose the farm. That's a family secret, so don't tell anyone I told you that, please."

"I promise I won't say a word," she replied, relocking the shop.

"Where would you like to go for supper?" Cliff asked as he closed her passenger door.

"Wherever you would like to go as long as it doesn't have sushi or a vegetarian only menu," Sage said.

"Meat and potatoes?"

"Sounds good to me. Or seafood, seafood is good, too," she replied, smiling.

"I know it's not fancy, but how about the diner? The food is good, and I like to support the local businesses."

"I love the diner. Can we make a quick stop at my mom's shop on the way by so I can tell her I'm going back to Moosehead tomorrow? I promise it will only take five minutes," Sage requested.

"No problem. I haven't seen your mom since last Christmas at the town party. And I don't think I've been to her shop for a couple of years."

The parking lot at *This and That* was packed, and Cliff had to park out on the road. As they walked to the shop, people were passing them with full bags of things they had purchased. There were people everywhere in the shop, hands full and still shopping, and a line of customers waiting to check out at the register.

"Mom, what is going on in here?" Sage asked,

standing next to the counter and bagging a customer's purchases.

"Cliff Fulton! How nice to see you. How are your parents doing?"

"Hello, Mrs. Fletcher. They're doing fine, thank you."

"Sarah, please. As for what is happening here, Mrs. Snow called me today and told me all the new things that would be arriving for my shop, so I decided to have a ten-dollar fill-a-bag sale. Word got out, and it's been crazy all day."

An argument broke out at the back of the shop. Edna Collins and another woman that Sage didn't know were arguing over an item that they each wanted.

"Let them go at it," Sarah said. "They'll figure it out."

A short time later, the two women had settled their problem, and of course Edna had won out. They came and joined the line at the register waiting to pay.

"I stopped in to tell you I'm going back to Moosehead tomorrow for a second load of items. The workshop is really filling up with everything I unloaded today and will be packed solid tomorrow night. I have sorted your things from mine, and they're on separate sides of the workshop."

"Sounds like you may need to use some of my storage area out back or you won't have any space to get any work done."

"That's the truth," Cliff said, smiling.

"I might take you up on that offer for some of the bigger pieces of furniture. And you need to clear out your display case for some signed first edition books I got for your shop."

"Really? First editions? And the family didn't want them?"

"No, I checked, and they didn't. I also got a box of yearbooks from Cupston and Moosehead high schools from around the time you went to school. I figured you might enjoy going through them and reminiscing. I know a lot of people in the area lost their yearbooks in the flood twenty years ago, and maybe they can find the year they graduated and replace them."

"What a great idea. Now, aren't you two supposed to be out on a date?"

"Mom, really?"

"Don't really me. Skedaddle. I can handle this crowd; I have all day. It was nice seeing you again, Cliff."

"You too, Mrs. Fletcher, ah, Sarah. Don't work too hard," Cliff replied.

It was past the supper rush when the couple arrived at the diner. Clair met them at the door and showed them to a secluded booth at the back of the patio room. She winked at Sage as she lit the candle on their table and walked away giving them some time to decide what they would be ordering.

At first, there was an awkward silence between the two. Sage was glad that she had the excuse of perusing the menu versus trying to come up with something to talk about. It seemed Cliff felt just as edgy as she did. Sage finally broke the silence.

"Don't let Claire and her romantic candle make you nervous. Her and Gabby have been after me to get out in the dating scene again since my breakup with Perry. I was just looking forward to a nice dinner and some adult conversation and nothing more, so don't feel pressured," Sage said.

"That makes me feel a lot better," he replied, letting out a deep breath.

"Good. Now what are we going to eat?"

Sage decided to order the pork chops and home-made applesauce along with mashed potatoes and summer squash. Cliff ordered the fisherman's platter with onion rings.

"I have never seen anyone order the platter here

and finish the whole thing in one sitting," Sage said. "Do you plan on doing that?"

'No, but I enjoy the variety of seafood they give you and I always end up taking some home for lunch the next day," he replied.

Sage's cell phone buzzed.

"I'm sorry, but I have to check this in case it's my mom."

She pulled up her messages. Gabby had texted her to tell her she couldn't go to Moosehead the following day. Rory had fallen from the roof of the house they were building, and although he didn't break anything, she had to stay with him for twenty-four hours in case of a concussion. Sage messaged her back and told her not to worry about it, to concentrate on taking care of Rory, and that she hoped he felt better.

"Is everything okay?" Cliff asked when she put her cell phone back in her purse.

"Gabby can't go with me tomorrow. Rory had an accident, and she has to stay with him. He's okay, nothing broken, but they have to watch him since he banged his head in the fall."

"Do you need another set of hands? I'm free tomorrow, and I can go with you and help," Cliff offered.

"I can't ask you to spend your day off moving stuff for me," Sage replied.

"Why not? I can move the furniture while you load the smaller items."

"It would be helpful. I do have some bigger pieces to move that would be easier with two people doing it. Are you sure you don't mind?"

"I haven't been to Moosehead for a while either. Boy, I guess I don't get out much," he said, laughing. "What time do you want to go?"

"I can pick you up on the way out of Cupston. I have to go right by the farm. How about nine o'clock?"

"It's a date. Well, you know what I mean," he said, smiling.

Sage looked at Cliff. He was ruggedly handsome, and his whole face lit up when he smiled. She was glad that she said yes to their date.

The rest of the evening passed quickly as the two became more comfortable with each other. Their conversations were centered around their families and what had happened in their own lives since they graduated high school. What Sage liked the most was the fact that they both enjoyed mysteries and thrillers and had read many of the same books.

After dinner, Cliff surprised her and took her to

the Dalton Dairy Stand for some homemade ice cream. He had a triple decker scoop of cherry vanilla in a waffle cone, and she enjoyed a double scoop of watermelon sherbet. He grabbed a handful of napkins, and Sage teased him about taking so many. But on a warm summer night, the ice cream melted faster than they could eat it, and almost all of the napkins had been used when they finally finished.

A little after ten, they pulled into Sage's driveway. He opened the truck door for her and walked her to her door. He was a true gentleman and gave her a quick peck on the cheek as he thanked her for a nice evening. She was glad it was nighttime, and he couldn't see her blushing when it happened. He said he would be ready to go in the morning, hopped in his truck, and drove off.

Sage got ready for bed and was feeling butterflies dancing in her stomach. She tried to pass it off in her mind as eating too much food over the course of the evening, but she knew Cliff was the one making her stomach flutter, and she hadn't felt like that in a long time. Crawling into bed, she fell asleep smiling.

Sage beeped the horn as she passed her mom's shop and saw Sarah and Flora sitting out front enjoying a morning cup of coffee. It really bothered her that the two women were spending so much time together. The sheriff still didn't know who had killed Ralph, and it could have very well been Flora.

Cliff was standing at the gate to the farm when Sage pulled up. He had a wooden picnic basket with him. Climbing into the front seat, he set the basket at his feet and closed the van door.

"Good morning! Are we ready to move some furniture?"

"You're awfully cheery this morning," Sage said, putting the van in gear.

"Why wouldn't I be? The sun is out, I'm going on an adventure, and my mother packed us a full picnic basket of great food. Check these out," he said, reaching into the basket. "Cinnamon apple muffins. Still warm and as big as softballs."

"I don't think I've ever seen a muffin as big as that one," Sage said, smiling at Cliff's enthusiasm. "I brought coffee. Yours is in the cup holder."

"How do you know how I like my coffee?"

"You had some at the diner last night. I watched how you fixed it before you drank it."

"Oh, yeah. Am I to assume that with all the mysteries you read that you notice everything around you?" he teased.

"Not everything … just mostly everything," she answered.

He put a muffin on a paper plate, broke it in half, and set it on the console between the seats for Sage.

"You weren't kidding. They are still warm," she said, taking a bite.

"My mom is up every morning baking for the farm hands. She feeds them breakfast before they go out into the fields or whatever they have to do that day. These are my favorites. The chunks of apples are from our own trees in the back orchard."

"I love to come apple picking in the fall at your farm. Honey Crisp is my favorite."

"The good weather and the ample amount of rain we have had so far this summer is going to offer up a big crop of apples this year. And pumpkins for the Fall."

"These are delicious. I'll have to get the recipe from your mom."

"I don't know if she'll part with her secret recipes, but you can ask."

"I can be very persuasive when I need to be," Sage replied.

"I'm sure you can, but you haven't faced anyone like my mom yet."

The remainder of the trip was filled with good-humored banter. They finally arrived at their destination and got right to work loading the van. The larger pieces of furniture were loaded first and everything else was fit in like putting a puzzle together. Two hours later, the van was filled to its busting point for the second time in as many days. Sage found even more items that she hadn't planned to take, but because she had room in the van, she squeezed them in. Mrs. Snow told her to take one more stroll through the house to make sure she hadn't missed anything that she wanted.

Cliff went through the remaining books that were left in the living room, took an armload to the van, and set them next to the picnic basket on the front seat floor. Mr. Snow flagged Sage down and handed her an old plane that he found in the shed in the backyard. He requested that she give it to Gabby since she had been looking for old tools the previous day.

Sage gave both the Snows big hugs and thanked them again for both her and her mother. She wished them luck selling the house and was informed that it was already spoken for and would be sold as soon as it was emptied. They gave Cliff a hug and told him to send love to his parents from them.

The trip home was a little slower than it was going since Sage was trying not to jostle the contents of the van around. They pulled over next to a small pond halfway home and enjoyed a wonderful lunch of fried chicken and potato salad along with a thermos of ice-cold lemonade. They walked around the edge of the lake watching the ducks as they swam around.

Sage watched Cliff as he talked to the ducks like they understood what he was saying to them. She had never felt as comfortable or at ease with Perry as she did with Cliff. Maybe she should have listened to Gabby a little sooner, but she would never admit that to her best friend. And besides, her grandmother was a firm believer that when the time was right, it would happen. Maybe now, the time was right for Sage to move on with her life.

Cliff had insisted that he ride to Sage's shop and help her unload the bigger pieces of furniture before she took him home. She relented, and they pulled into her driveway up to the front of the workshop. She turned off the van and sat staring forward.

"What's the matter?" Cliff asked.

"This can't be good," she answered.

CHAPTER FOUR

Sage stopped at the door of her workshop, giving Cliff the time to catch up with her. The padlock was on the ground, and the door was open a few inches.

"It looks like someone paid your shop a visit while you were gone. You did lock it before you left this morning, didn't you?"

"I locked it last night. I didn't go into the shop this morning, but I would have noticed the padlock on the ground when I got in the van," she replied.

"Let me go in first and make sure no one is still in there," Cliff suggested.

"Be careful," she replied. "I'm going to call the sheriff."

"They're gone," Cliff said, exiting the building.

"The dispatcher said not to touch anything, and

they would get here as soon as they could. I'm going to walk around inside and see if anything has been moved or taken," Sage said.

Cliff followed her inside. Sage walked around but didn't see anything moved or missing. A soft knock sounded at the door. Deputy Andy Bell was standing there waving them outside.

"What's up?" he asked as they joined him.

"Someone broke into my workshop while we were in Moosehead today," Sage replied. "The lock has been picked and is lying there on the ground."

"Is anything missing?"

"Not that I can tell. Then again, I just tossed everything inside yesterday when I unloaded the van. But doesn't it seem funny that this lock was picked just like my mom's lock was picked at her shop?"

"Do you think the two events are related?" Cliff asked.

"I do. If we find the person who can pick locks, we may find who killed Ralph. But what would they want in my shop?"

"Who knew you weren't going to be here today?" Deputy Bell asked.

"Gabby, my mom, and half the town that was in her shop yesterday when I told her," Sage replied.

"That's no help," Bell replied. "I'll take the lock

and see if we can get any prints off it. You need to go through the shop again and see if you can figure out if and what they took."

"Do you have another lock that you can use?" Cliff asked.

"I do. Before I unload the van, I'm going to look around again to see what's missing. You don't have to stay. It may take a while before I get to the point of unloading," Sage said to Cliff.

"I'm taking the lock and heading back to the station. Call if you figure out what's gone," Bell said, putting the lock into a clear evidence bag and sealing it.

"I'll take you home before I get busy in the work-shop," Sage said.

"I'm not going anywhere. I'll stand guard while you poke around. You don't know if someone will come back or not, and I'm not leaving you out here by yourself," Cliff replied.

"You really don't have to stay," Sage insisted.

"I know I don't have to; I chose to. Now, let's find out what they broke in for."

They started on the side that held all Sage's items. After a short while, she could tell that nothing had been moved or was missing on her side. They moved to Sarah's side, which had more boxes and smaller items that they had to go through.

"I know what's missing!" she exclaimed, standing at the edge of a pile of boxes.

"What did they take?" Cliff asked, joining her.

"The box of yearbooks is missing," she replied.

"Why would anyone take those?" Cliff asked.

"I don't know, but that's what they took," she replied.

"That's crazy. Risk breaking in somewhere and getting caught for some old yearbooks?"

"Unless there's something in one of those books that someone doesn't want anyone to see," Sage said. "The day that Ralph was murdered, someone broke into the Peterson house and ransacked it while Flora was down at the police station being questioned. She told me the only things that were gone were some of Ralph's personal things. I wonder if his yearbooks were among the things taken?"

"It's too late to go ask her tonight."

"It is. I guess if you still are up to it, we can unload the van, and then I can run you home."

"It shouldn't take us too long. I'll start while you go inside and get the other padlock so we can lock up after we're done."

They emptied the van of everything but Gabby's

triple dresser. Sage locked the workshop and drove Cliff home. She promised him steaks on the grill the following weekend for all his help. It had been a long day, and she was exhausted. Returning home, she checked that the lock was secure on the workshop door and went into her house to go to bed.

This and That was closed. Sage had planned on spending the whole day in her own workshop sorting the items and loading the van with all the things that were going to her mother's shop on Tuesday when she went to work there. But her curiosity got the better of her, and she decided to make a trip to Flora Peterson's to ask her if Ralph's yearbooks had been stolen.

Gabby was so excited to get the triple dresser for her second bedroom. Rory hadn't left for work yet, and he and Sage moved the dresser upstairs. Sage tried to tell her friend about the break-in at her workshop, but Gabby was more interested in how the date went with Cliff. Her friend squealed with delight when she found out that Cliff had gone with her to Moosehead.

"Cliff and his family are good people," Rory said. "We graduated the same year, and I have known him since we went to kindergarten together. He could throw a mean football in high school."

"He seems really nice," Sage replied. "Next Sunday, I invited him for steaks on the grill as a thank you for him helping me yesterday. Do you two want to join us? I just bought that new patio set that we can christen."

"Sounds good to me. We'll bring the beer," Rory replied.

"How are you feeling by the way?" she asked.

"I'm fine. It was a stupid accident that shouldn't have happened. Luckily, I landed on soft grass and not on one of the piles of boards that were scattered around the work site."

"I'm glad you're okay. Have to run. Got lots to get accomplished today."

"Be careful. I don't like the fact that someone broke into your place," Gabby said, hugging her.

"You mean you actually heard me tell you about that?" Sage teased her friend.

"I did, and I will continue to worry until this whole mess is straightened out with you and your mom and they find Ralph's killer."

"Love you both," Sage yelled out the window of the van as she pulled away.

Parking the van at *This and That,* Sage walked over to Flora's house. Stepping up on the porch, she heard two people arguing inside. She waited to see if she could hear what they were saying, but the voices were too garbled. When she knocked on the door, the voices suddenly stopped. Flora answered the door, and Sage could see a man about Flora's age standing behind her.

"Can I help you? I'm a little busy right now, Sage."

"I just had a quick question," she replied, leaning closer to Flora. "Is that your attorney? He's quite handsome."

The older woman's face lit up, and her demeanor softened.

"Yes, he is," she whispered back. "This is Paul Tilson, my attorney. Paul this is Sarah's daughter, Sage."

"Nice to meet you," he said, sitting down on the hall bench.

"Is everything okay?' Sage asked.

"Oh, everything is fine. Paul just gave me some bad news about Ralph's life insurance. The company won't pay me the benefits until my name is cleared of his murder. Have you ever heard anything so ridiculous? They think I would kill my own…" Flora said, her voice trailing off. "Never mind. You don't need to hear about my troubles. What question did you need me to answer, dear?"

"The day you were at the police station, and someone ransacked your house, you said it was only Ralph's things that were missing. By any chance did Ralph still have his yearbooks and did the thief take them?"

"It's funny you asked that because that was one of the few things that were missing when I finally got the place straightened out and could do an inventory. His four yearbooks were among the missing items," Flora replied. "How did you know?"

"My workshop was broken into last night, and the only thing stolen was a box of old Cupston and Moosehead yearbooks. Someone doesn't want those books available for people to look through. I think they might tell us who killed Ralph or at least point us in the right direction."

Flora turned and looked at her attorney. He shook his head yes, and she turned back to Sage.

"You need to come sit on the porch. I have something I need to tell you," the older woman said, sighing deeply.

Sage sat in a wicker rocking chair while Flora and Paul sat on the porch swing together.

"I don't know where to begin, but here goes. Paul is my fiancé, not just my attorney. We have been engaged for six years. Ralph Peterson was my brother not my husband."

"I don't understand," Sage replied. "Why lie to everyone?"

"It's a long story. My father was a very controlling man, and as such, he drove my mother into an early grave. Years later, he died a wealthy man. In his will, he made the stipulation that I would live with Ralph until he found a suitable mate for me. Only then could I inherit my share of the estate. My father thought all women were fools and had no intelligence. We were put on this earth to be ruled over by men."

"That's rough," Sage said.

"It was. I met Paul, and we fell in love, but Ralph didn't approve of his profession and would not allow me to marry him. I really think it was because Paul was much smarter than Ralph and he stood up to my brother on my behalf. Ralph kept trying to force me to marry one of his no-good friends so all the money could stay in his control."

"Was the money worth being tied down like that?" Sage asked.

"Flora's share is a little over a million dollars. It was being held in a trust only to be released upon Ralph's approval or his death. Ralph's share of the estate combined with Flora's is worth over five million dollars. The life insurance is another half a million."

"That would make for a definite motive to kill Ralph. That and him preventing you from marrying Paul," Sage stated.

"That is why we haven't said anything even after her brother's death. People would think the same way you are right now," Paul said.

"Flora would be a very wealthy woman with her brother out of the way."

"All I have really wanted was my share and to spend the rest of my life with Paul, but Ralph was just like my father and had to be in control, no matter what."

"I think you need to call the sheriff and tell him what you just told me. If it comes from you first and you're honest and open about everything with him, he may not look at you so suspiciously if it comes up in his investigation. I'm not saying he'll let you off the hook, but it may help with the trust issue later on down the road."

"I think she's right, Flora. We need to call the sheriff and tell him."

"The two of you grew up in Moosehead, right? What year did you both graduate?"

"Let's see. I graduated in 1978 from Moosehead

High School. Ralph graduated in 1975."

"So, I need to find a copy of each of the four years that Ralph was in high school and start to go through them. Someone doesn't want their picture seen because it would connect them to your brother. Did your brother ever date anyone seriously?"

"He had many girlfriends in high school. But after my father died, Ralph was more interested in all the money he had and controlling my life. I don't know of anyone he might have been seeing, but then again, he never let me leave the house. I would have had no connection to the outside world if Paul hadn't bought me a cell phone and paid the monthly bill so Ralph didn't know I had it. I kept the phone hidden in my room, and we would talk whenever Ralph left the house. It kept me sane."

"Please don't say anything to anyone about what you have learned today. It will eventually come out, but maybe we can control how and when it does," Paul requested.

"I won't say a word. But you really need to call the sheriff because if anyone does find out, this is a small town, and you know how fast gossip can spread," Sage replied. "Now, I am heading to the Cupston Public Library. I need to check out some yearbooks from the archives. I will ask the same of you. Please don't mention the yearbook situation to anyone until I can check out my theory."

"Anything you can do to help Flora will be greatly appreciated. My girl needs some joy in her life. She deserves it after all she has been through," Paul said, grabbing hold of her hand and squeezing it tightly. "If I can help in any way, just let me know."

"You just stay with your fiancée. This person may believe that Flora might know who they are, and she could be the next target. I'll be in touch if I learn anything. Please call the sheriff."

"We are going to do that right now," Paul said, standing up. "Please be careful as well. This person might not like you nosing around."

Sage walked back to her van and sat in the parking lot.

This opens up a whole new direction for suspects. Any of Ralph's friends could have wanted money that was promised to them if they married Flora, and when they didn't get it, they took their revenge out on Ralph.

The Cupston Public Library was a small, two-story building on the outskirts of town. Cora Hurtle had been the head librarian there for over forty years. She knew everyone in town and kept many secrets that the locals had confided in her. The library was well organized, and Cora knew where every book or research paper was located. She was a wealth of information.

Sage walked up to the counter and slid her books in the return slot at the end of the desk. She had been meaning to return them but hadn't gotten around to it. There were very few people in the library, so Sage felt safe talking to Cora at the desk.

"Here to get more mysteries?" Cora asked.

"Not today. I'm looking for something totally different," Sage replied. "Does the library still have the yearbook section in the archives?"

"We do. It's still downstairs, but the books have been moved to the smaller area at the back. Exactly what are you looking for?"

"I'm looking for Moosehead High's books from 1972 to 1975. I know we have all of Cupston's books, but do we have a complete set of Moosehead's books?"

"They are all down there. Right up to last year's graduating classes for both towns."

"Can they be checked out or do they have to remain in the building?' Sage asked.

"Technically, they are classified as research books, especially the earlier books from the late 1800s and early 1900s. And after the flood, not many locals had their own books left, so they come here for reunion information and such. But I trust you, and if you need to take them home, I'm sure you will take good care of them and return them in the same condition that you borrowed them."

"Awesome. I'll be back," Sage said, heading for the stairs that led to the basement.

The yearbooks were filed by town and by year which made it easy for Sage to find the exact ones she needed. She took the four books and went back to the front desk to check them out.

"Mrs. Hurtle, did you graduate from Cupston or Moosehead?"

"I graduated from Cupston, but my husband, God rest his soul, graduated from Moosehead. Back then, the two high schools were pretty much inseparable. The population was much smaller then, and most people left the area after they graduated for better jobs elsewhere."

"So, you knew everyone from both schools?"

"That's how I met my Howard. We had many Saturday night school dances that included the students from both schools."

"Did you know Ralph Peterson back then?"

"Oh, my, no. I graduated a good twenty years before him and his class. I did know his mother, poor woman. She died way too early of a broken heart. Maybe not so much a broken heart but a broken spirit. Dottie never stood a chance against that husband of hers."

So, Flora's story is true.

"Thank you for all your help. I promise to get these back to you as soon as possible," Sage said.

"I trust you, dear, or I would never let them leave with you. Good luck finding Ralph's killer," Cora said, smiling.

"How did you know that's what I wanted them for?"

"Simple. You and mysteries go hand in hand. And I am positive you won't give up until you solve Ralph's murder. That's what all the questions are for, correct?"

"Correct! Just don't tell anyone what I'm up to," Sage requested.

"You know things don't stay secret around here for too long. By the way, how are things going with you and Cliff?" she asked, winking.

"Does the whole town know I went on a date with Cliff?" Sage asked.

"Yes, ma'am! It's no secret around here that he's had a thing for you for a long time. He's a good one. Hold on to him if you can."

"Thank you for the advice," Sage said, heading for the door. "See you in a few days."

Driving home, Sage saw the sheriff's car parked in Flora's driveway and decided to stop. They were on the front porch enjoying a glass of iced tea and talking. Flora looked almost relieved as she sipped her drink. Sheriff White thanked Sage for suggesting the couple call him and let him know what the truth was surrounding the brother and sister.

"I stopped because I had another question to ask you before I went home for the evening. Flora, how many people in Cupston knew that you and your brother had money and were well off?"

"No one as far as I know. That's why we moved here. After so many years of living elsewhere, we weren't known in Cupston anymore. Moosehead yes, by a select few that my brother had tried to marry me off to, but Cupston no. Why?"

"I'm just remembering a conversation I had with someone a while ago. Thank you for the information. I'm heading home now," Sage said, starting down the porch stairs.

"Hold on! What are you up to?" the sheriff asked. "And did you figure out what was taken out of your workshop yesterday?"

"Honestly, only one thing was taken," Sage replied. "A box of yearbooks."

"Didn't they take Ralph's yearbooks, too?" the sheriff asked Flora.

"His yearbooks, some financial papers, and some gold jewelry was missing."

"I think I need to go to the library and check out the yearbooks in question," the sheriff stated.

"Too late," Sage replied, smiling.

"You already have them, don't you?" he asked, frowning. "Seriously?"

"They're in the van as we speak. I was going home tonight to look through them. If you like I will bring them to the station tomorrow," Sage said.

"Or I could take them right now and charge you with interfering with a murder investigation," he replied.

"Really? You would do that?" Sage asked.

"I could, but I won't. I'll give you the night to look through them, but I want them at the station tomorrow morning by nine. Fair?"

"So fair! I'll see you then."

As she walked away, she heard the sheriff say to Flora that Sage had a great eye for detail and had an uncanny knack for solving mysteries. Sometimes he had to give her some space, and sometimes he had to put his foot down. It made Sage happy to know that the sheriff trusted her and her judgement.

Double-checking that all her doors were locked once she was home, she set the yearbooks on her kitchen table and poured herself a glass of wine. Starting with the one dated 1972, she went page by page studying faces and names. Ralph Peterson's picture was listed in the freshman class, but after going through the entire book, no one else stuck out to her.

Refilling her wine glass and throwing a beef pot pie into the oven, she started on the next book dated 1973. This time, Ralph's picture was under the sophomore listings and in the junior varsity football team picture. In several other pictures, Ralph was captured with a pretty female, but there was no listing of her name. They looked happy together. Sage searched the younger classmen pictures but could not find the girl anywhere.

By 1974, Ralph's picture was splattered all throughout the book. The football team, basketball captain, and debate team were a few of the activities that he was involved in. He was still dating the same girl, and they appeared together in several pictures. Sage looked a little closer at the pictures, and she seemed somewhat familiar to her.

Flora first appeared in the 1975 yearbook under the freshman listings. It was apparent that the brother and sister must have been still getting along back then since Ralph left his legacy listing to his younger sister wishing her all the best while she was in high school.

It was also the first time that the girl he had been dating during high school was identified by name. It was a group prom picture. Ralph and his date were wearing crowns. It was only her first name but that was all that Sage needed.

That explains why I couldn't find her in any of the other yearbooks. She wasn't from Moosehead, she was from Cupston. It's time to get some answers.

The buzzer went off signaling her pot pie was done cooking. She took it out of the oven to let it cool a bit while she locked the yearbooks in her wall safe. Finishing off the bottle of wine, she ate her supper in front of the television and then went to bed.

The next morning, she walked into the police station and requested to speak to the sheriff. Deputy Bell showed her to the back office, opened the door for her, and announced her arrival.

"I think I know why Ralph was killed and who did it. I just need to figure out a way to prove it," she said, setting the books down on the sheriff's desk. "I think we need to set a trap using these."

"Interesting. Tell me what you propose."

Sage laid out a plan that she had concocted while she lay in bed the previous night. The sheriff was in total agreement but wanted to see it play out before he agreed with her on who the killer was and why. She left the police station and put their plan into action.

Once inside the town hall, she went directly to the town clerk's office. Edna was sitting behind her desk mindlessly shuffling around a pile of papers while staring out into space. Sage stood there for a minute or so before clearing her throat to alert Edna she was standing there. She looked up and sprang to her feet hurrying toward the counter.

"What can I do for you today, Sage?"

"I'm purchasing a storage trailer for my back yard, and I need the proper paperwork for a permit," Sage replied.

"I can get that for you. There's a twenty-five-dollar fee that has to accompany the application when you return it," Edna replied, pulling some papers out of a drawer in front of her. "You have to have the maps of your property pulled to show where the septic system and utility lines run so the trailer won't be set down on top of them."

"Great. My little shop has become too crowded to

work in, and I need somewhere to store the bigger pieces of furniture until I can get to them."

"You're lucky you don't have any close neighbors that will complain about the trailer," Edna said, handing her the needed paperwork. "Your dad looked for months for just the right house for your graduation present. He said he would find you a place with a workshop for your new business, and he did. Some men know how to step up and keep their word."

"Yea, I won't have to go through what my mom did with Ralph Peterson. Speaking of Ralph, the talk around town is the sheriff may have a lead as to who killed him."

"Really? You don't say," Edna said.

"It was weird. He was telling me when Ralph's house was broken into his yearbooks were stolen, and the same thing happened at my shop. It was broken into the other day, and the only thing taken was a box of old yearbooks. The sheriff figures someone doesn't want something in the books to be seen."

"That's interesting. What does he think he will find?"

"I have no idea. He told me he was going to the library after lunch to check the same yearbooks out of the archives that would have been at Ralph's house. It will be interesting to see what he does find if anything at all. It seems pretty far-fetched to me."

"The sheriff is usually pretty spot on in his thinking," Edna said. "Is there anything else I can help you with?"

"No, I think this will do for now, thank you. If you can point me in the direction of where I can obtain a copy of my property map, I would appreciate it. The trailer is being delivered next week, so I need to get home and fill this out to get my permit in time before the delivery."

"Third door down on the left. Carl will be glad to help you," Edna said, smiling. "Have a good day."

Sage walked down the hall in the direction Edna sent her, but instead of going into the accessor's office, she ducked into the bathroom. From this vantage point she could see both the clerk's office and the side exit out of the building.

Keeping the door open a tiny crack, Sage kept an eye on Edna's office. Ten minutes later, the town clerk exited her office, locked it, and flipped the sign on the door that said she would return in an hour. As she strutted up the hallway, she headed right for the bathroom where Sage was hiding. The young woman took a few steps back and was running an excuse in her head if Edna walked in on her.

"How many times have I told these people to close the door after they are done in here?" she muttered as she reached for the doorknob.

Sage stood perfectly still not wanting to make any noise. She heard the bar being pushed to open the exit door and let out her breath. Taking out her cell phone she sent a message.

I believe the rat is coming for the cheese.

CHAPTER FIVE

Sage made sure Edna had left the parking lot before she exited the town hall. She knew the sheriff was already in place hiding down in the archive's small office. He would be able to see Edna as she flipped through the yearbooks looking for the ones that had already been removed.

Taking the long way around to the library, Sage pulled into the parking lot and picked a spot the furthest away she could get from Edna's car. Not wanting to be seen, she entered the library and took a seat near the magazine racks to the left of the front desk. Mrs. Hurtle acknowledged her with a slight nod and went back to what she was doing.

Loud screaming could be heard coming from downstairs. Sage jumped out of her chair, and along with Mrs. Hurtle, they ran to the top of the stairs and waited. Sheriff White was escorting Edna up the stairs. She was screaming in protest about the way she was being treated.

"Do you know who I am?" she yelled. "My family owns a good percentage of this town. You can't treat me this way."

"Hush up!" the sheriff ordered.

"You! You set me up!" Edna said, lunging at Sage.

"Oh, no you don't," the sheriff said, restraining her and physically pushing her down in a chair that was close by the top of the stairs.

"I didn't set you up, Edna. I just repeated a conversation that I had with someone. You took it upon yourself to react to what I said," Sage replied.

"What were you looking for in the yearbook section?" the sheriff asked.

Edna crossed her arms in front of her and closed her eyes. Sage held her finger to her lips and the sheriff nodded.

"He crossed you, didn't he Edna? He lied to you all these years, making you think he would marry you and you would live the good life as his wife," Sage said.

She opened her eyes and then closed them again.

"You were high school sweethearts. And then when he inherited all his family's money, he dumped you, didn't he?"

A tear slid down Edna's cheek.

"After all those years that you waited for him, he told you the money was more important to him than you were. Did he tell you that women were inferior and were meant to serve men? He turned out to be just like his father, didn't he?"

"He promised me he would marry me when he moved back to Cupston. Every time he came into my office to file a complaint, he would tell me soon; we will get married soon. He strung me along so I would do his bidding even though I knew the complaints were bogus and would go nowhere. Then I found out that he was telling everyone that Flora was his wife and not his sister. He wouldn't let Flora be on her own because he would lose control of her portion of the estate."

"But he told Flora that their father stated in the will that he had to choose her husband and that he would always have control of the money," Sage replied.

"That's not true. I have the real will that Ralph kept hidden from everyone. I took it the night I broke into the house. Flora was free to marry who she wanted to and when she did, she was to receive her portion of the estate. It was a much smaller amount than her brother's but hers nonetheless."

"What a slimeball he was," Sage said, egging the woman on.

"He was," she said, wiping away a tear.

"What happened, Edna? Tell us about the night Ralph died," Sage asked.

"He was going to one of his bowling tournaments, and I was waiting outside in the side yard for him to come out. I called him over to where I was to confront him about marrying me. He laughed at me and called me a stupid woman."

"That made you mad, didn't it?" Sage asked.

"Mad isn't the word for it. He insulted me further by saying he would rather pay a woman of the night than let me spend a cent of his money. He was laughing so hard at his own words that my blood boiled. All I could think of was all those wasted years that I'd waited for him and spent alone."

"Then what happened?" Cora asked.

"He bent over to pick up his suitcase, still laughing at me, and I picked up a nearby rock and whacked him on the head with it. I was so enraged that I didn't realize what I had done until after it was done. He didn't move, and he wasn't breathing.

I panicked and dragged his body behind their garage."

"But Flora saw him pull out of the driveway," Sage said.

"It was me driving the car. I parked it up the street and returned to the house. I had to buy some time to hide the body. Later, I moved the car to my old barn."

"Did someone help you move the body to the trailer?" the sheriff asked.

"No! It took me most of the night, but I eventually got Ralph to the door of the trailer."

"Who picked the lock?" Sage asked.

"I did. My dad was a master locksmith, and I learned a thing or two growing up with him. Padlocks are easy to open."

"Why my mom's trailer? Why didn't you just leave Ralph behind the garage to be found there?" Sage asked.

"Because I knew there was bad blood between your mom and Ralph, and if he was found in a locked trailer, her locked trailer, the sheriff's investigation would lean that way. And poor Flora had been through enough in her lifetime that I didn't want to put any suspicion on her if the body had been found behind their garage."

"I guess that's everything. Come on, Edna, it's

time to go to the station," the sheriff said, assisting her up from the chair. "I won't cuff you if you promise you won't cause any trouble."

"Ladies, I will need you to come to the station and file a full report for me," the sheriff said to Cora and Sage. "Either today or tomorrow will be fine."

"Sage, please tell your mother I am so sorry for what I did. I wasn't thinking straight that night when I did what I did."

"I'll tell her," Sage promised.

"Come on, Sheriff. I've spent my whole life alone, and now I will spend the rest of it alone in a jail cell," Edna mumbled.

They watched out the front door of the library as the sheriff placed Edna in the back of the patrol car and drove away. Anyone that had heard the confession had to have some sympathy for Edna. Cora shook her head and closed the door.

"I never expected when I let you take the yearbooks home that something like this would happen right in front of my eyes. By the way, where are the books?" Cora asked.

"They're at the police station in the sheriff's office. I'm sure he will return them to you as soon as he's done with them," Sage replied. "Now I have to get to *This and That* before my mother finds out that I opened the shop four hours late."

"I won't say a word," Cora said, smiling.

Sage arrived at her mother's shop to see it open and the parking lot mostly full. She took a deep breath and walked toward the door expecting to be lectured on her responsibilities. Sarah was behind the register, smiling and chatting with the customers. Sage stood just inside the door watching her mother.

"Don't just stand there. Grab a bag and get to work," Sarah yelled to her daughter.

"How did you know I wouldn't be here?" she asked as she bagged the customer's purchases.

"Sheriff White called me this morning and told me about the little plan that you had come up with. He agreed with your reasoning and thought you were right about who the killer was. So, I came into work until you got here."

"You're awesome, Mom."

"I didn't solve the murder, you did. And it's all over town that you did, and that's why it's so busy here. But thank you for clearing my name. And I'd like you to turn around and meet my newest employee, Flora Peterson, soon to be Flora Tilson."

"I'm just volunteering right now. I like to spend time talking to people and having a social life. Paul and I have decided to stay in the house next door, but we are going to make lots of changes to the property. Happy changes."

"I am so happy for you, Flora," Sage said, hugging her.

"I even asked your mother if she wanted to take on a partner. We could build a whole new addition onto the back of the building to enlarge the display area. She's thinking about it," Flora said. "Paul said it would be a good investment."

"I have a proposition for you, my daughter. I'll stay here the rest of the day if you will come in tomorrow and work so I can have a full day off."

"That actually works out better because I never had a chance to load the van with all your items from the Snows' aunt's house. I can go home and do that now so it will be ready to be unloaded here tomorrow."

"Sounds good. I'll see you then," Sarah said.

As the week progressed, things returned to normal. Sage was interviewed for the local paper, and her dad called her to say how proud of her he was. After a few days, the whole Ralph Peterson thing was all but a memory. There was some truth to Sage's plan since she did fill out the paperwork and order a new storage trailer that was delivered and tucked in next to the row of trees at the back of her property.

Sunday morning, Sage was out in her back yard hosing down the patio set and picnic table for the cookout. The propane tank had been checked the previous day and was three-quarters full. Four large cuts of New York sirloin steaks were defrosting on the kitchen counter. A cooler full of ice was sitting on the deck waiting for the beer that Rory was going to add to it when he arrived.

Making potato salad, Sage couldn't help but think about seeing Cliff again. It would be nice not to be the third wheel when it came to spending time with Rory and Gabby. Cliff seemed so easygoing, and Sage liked that about him. As she daydreamed, a knock sounded on the front door.

"Anyone home?" Cliff yelled.

"Back here in the kitchen. Come on in," she replied.

"I come bearing gifts. Fresh from the farm," he said, holding up a bag of corn on the cob and another bag of monstrous bright red tomatoes.

"These are huge," Sage said, holding up a tomato. "I bet these are going to taste great in a salad."

"What can I do to help?" he asked.

"Pull up a stool and talk to me while I finish preparing the side dishes."

"Congratulations on solving Ralph's murder. I can't believe you figured it out just from the yearbook pictures," Cliff said, stealing a piece of pickle off the cutting board.

"It wasn't just that. It was different little things that Edna said over the last week."

"Like what?"

"When I was at the diner, she picked a fight with me. One of her statements was about how rich people needed to be held accountable for their actions. No one around Cupston knew that Ralph was rich, and I didn't catch it until several days later."

"What else?"

"I think I already had it figured out, but at the town hall that morning, she was talking about my dad and made the statement that at least some men keep their word and promises. I knew she was talking about Ralph, and it kind of sealed the deal for me."

"Well, you did a fine job, Miss Detective. I'm very proud of you," Cliff replied. "I guess reading all those crime novels finally paid off."

"It sure did," she said, covering the potato salad and setting it in the fridge. "How about we play a round of horseshoes while we wait for Gabby and Rory to get here?"

"Are you any good?" Cliff asked.

"Am I any good? My dad and I took the town championship two years in a row at the Fourth of July town picnic."

"Sounds like stiff competition. We'll see how good you are. Let's make a bet. You win, I cook the steaks, I win, you have to go out on a second date with me."

"Let's go. You better try really hard if you want a second date with me," Sage teased, already knowing that a second date, a third, and many more was what she wanted to happen in her future.

***

If you enjoyed Bed and Buried and are looking for more Trash to Treasure adventures, check out Chair-Ish the Thought, today!

Printed in Great Britain
by Amazon

25806274R00078